I0584349

# Praise for Far from Home

Sometimes terrifying, often poignant—the twelve stories of *Far From Home* by Vincent Meis depict the ways we humans can be estranged from that place we are most comfortable, whether it is within us or situated on a map. Whether to Cuba, the Middle East, or a high school reunion, each protagonist leaves but also remains tethered to where or what they left. Well worth reading!

—Richard May, author of *Gay All Year*

The characters in Vincent Traughber Meis's collection of short stories experience both the dangers and thrills of being strangers in a strange land, gay in conservative cultures, which make their trials all the more difficult. They encounter violence and confusion, but also sweetness in their adventures through the Middle East, Cuba, Mexico and beyond. Most importantly, they learn unsettling things about themselves and are forever changed by their journeys. Be prepared to be moved, surprised, and shaken by the adversities of people unmoored from the places they call home. *Far from Home* is a superb addition to LGBTQ literature, and Meis has a true knack for bringing exotic places to life.

—Rob Rosen, author of *Genie in a Vodka Bottle*

# FAR FROM HOME

*Vincent Traughber Meis*

A NineStar Press Publication

www.ninestarpress.com

# Far from Home

ISBN: 978-1-64890-400-4

First Edition, October, 2021

Also available in eBook, ISBN: 978-1-64890-399-1

CONTENT WARNING:
This book contains sexual content, which may only be suitable for mature readers. Depictions of addiction, cheating, death of a loved one, depression, drug addiction, grief, guns, homophobia, murder, graphic violence, and rape.

# Man in a Shalwar Kameez

It's a coffee-colored afternoon: thick, murky, unsweetened, bitter, poured in a long stream from a *dallah,* hot but cooling rapidly. The air is the color of cardamom seeds, their skin, their eyes. This time of day the same dull brown coats the inside of his head after a rising time of 4:30 a.m., fumbling in darkness to strangle the alarm. He sees the days, weeks, months stretched out in front of him, a path paved in riyals, leading him through the wan desert and, he hopes, toward an oasis. Or is it only a mirage? How much longer does he have to be in the Kingdom? He glances at his watch, calculating the amount of money he has made in the last hour, a pittance compared to the CEO of the international company he works for, though for him and his pre-Saudi life, a fortune.

A thunderstorm that morning flashed out of the murky sky, pummeling this flat wide expanse of beach with a long rain. Rainstorms in the desert are a new phenomenon for him. For days a ceiling has pressed down lower and lower, alternately dropping and holding back its holy water, instantly sullied by its touching of the land. A chain of dirty puddles formed upon a resistant ground, hurrying to stagnation, calling mosquitoes to come perform their pagan rituals of breeding. Garbage, carried by the wind, strewn across the sand, has summoned flies and maggot producers of all types. He steps gingerly toward the sea, avoiding broken bottles and rusting cans, happily less vulnerable in his sneakers than the Saudis in their sandals.

His eyes squint against the gritty air, and pluck from this soiled landscape a man of fine features, an apparition, his white *shalwar kameez* fluttering in the breeze, bushy dark hair uncovered, not Saudi, Urdu speaker most likely by his attire. But he is real. His beckoning smile cleans the air and calms the American's rancor, transforming it to the far more dangerous trap of desire. What had he been angry about? He doesn't remember. No doubt a minor annoyance due to an inexplicable part of his host country's culture.

"Hello," the man says, tugging lightly on his thick mustache. "Where you from?"

"American, and you?"

"Pakistani. I am Adil."

They shake hands. "I'm Mark."

Adil releases his hand and touches his heart. "Nice to meet you," he says in a beguiling accent. The sun attempts to burn its way through the cloud cover, but the Pakistani's black eyes are already shining, providing light. "What you do?"

"Just walking."

"Me, too. Watch out." He points out a piece of glass. He's wearing dressy black boots. "My day off I come here to visit friends."

"From where?"

"Jubail. I work there. And you?"

"I'm at the Navy base. I teach English."

"Oh, maybe you help me with my English." Eyebrows rise high above his smile, white teeth, suggesting an exchange of some sort. "We go have coffee?"

"Yes, but please, no Arabic coffee."

"Ha ha. Maybe you like it sweet."

They walk back to the corniche and cross to the shopping center on the other side. Just inside the entrance to the bustling center with a lofty roof of skylights is a café, tables between planters filled with lush plastic plants. They order cappuccinos and sit in the male section separated from the smaller family section where several women sit, black shadows of human form you can see through the latticework dividers if you are so inclined.

Adil glances toward the family section. "Are you married?"

It is always one of the first questions. Trick question. Mark wonders what the correct answer is. He can say he was, but he's divorced now. Or never married. He decides on a simple no. "And you?"

"Not yet. I work here to finish my contract, then I go back and get married." He shows his pearly white teeth again. He's old enough to have crow's feet, a few strands of gray in his hair. He wears the kameez open halfway down, his hairy chest peeking above his tank top.

A man in Western clothes, Mediterranean looks, passes by, looks up, and shouts an angry threat. The pigeon takes flight as do several others who have been cooing on the rafters. The man goes to the counter and asks for a napkin, brushes his shoulder. Adil laughs.

"Maybe is good luck for him," Adil says. "Let's go for a drive. Prayer call is coming."

"You have a car?"

"Yes. You surprised?"

"No. That's cool." Mark, despite being much higher in the hierarchy of foreign workers, relies on public transportation. As they exit, Adil puts his hand lightly on Mark's lower back, entreating him to go first out of the cool into heat. The sun has made a brief appearance but is dropping behind the layer of haze, perpetually lounging on the horizon. They walk side by side. High in the minaret a speaker crackles and a voice begins. It is the Asr prayer call.

"You don't go to the mosque?"

Adil turns to Mark with a smirk. "Not today."

"Why not today?"

"Because I meet a new friend."

Movement surrounds them as shops close. Screeching metal doors slide down tight tracks cutting through the damp air, sounding like screams until they are drowned by the sudden shot-like explosion of the fully extended doors striking the pavement. From across the street comes the clang of gates brought together and the eerie rattle of a chain joining them in a clumsy embrace. The sounds echo up and down the block as a car speeds by on the corniche, honking at each intersection sending shadowy figures scurrying, gripping more tightly the plastic shopping bags dangling from their wrists. Men duck into cars and alleys as the scarves on their heads flap with the sudden haste.

"Come on," says Adil as he picks up the pace, and a short time later stops at a car. "Ta da!" It is not pretty. The white Nissan is several years old and suffering from the sea air. "This is my baby. Don't laugh."

They get on the road out into the desert. Mark has no idea where they're going or if he'll ever make it back, something he tries not to think about as he sits in the death seat with a mad Pakistani at the wheel. Adil reaches over and opens the glove compartment. "Look in there. Poems I wrote. Go ahead. Look."

Mark takes the rumpled papers out and looks at them, and then at the road that Adil is not watching. Adil's eyes return to the road, and he pulls into the passing lane. He floors the Nissan.

"I can't read the poems. Is this Arabic?"

"Similar. It is my language, Urdu. I can translate for you." He leans over and focuses on the lines, says something about the stars of heaven and tasting bliss and hearts bursting, but Mark can't concentrate because he is petrified at Adil's lack of attention to the road. Mark yelps as they rapidly come up on the car in front of them at the same moment he realizes the car has no seatbelts. Adil stomps on the brake, and Mark grabs the dashboard. "Okay, I tell you later."

Soon all the buildings are behind them, and they plunge into vast open space, the car rattling along at speeds that feel impossible for the small car. Adil thrusts his hand into a haphazard pile of homemade cassettes between the seats and jams one into the player. Pakistani disco music with pounding percussion, synthesizers, and wiggly notes blasts Mark's chest.

Mark wonders why he is always attracted to extreme people even though they scare the shit out of him. Is it the thrill of being close to the edge like that time he tried amyl nitrate, the heart-pumping feeling of being alive?

Adil's torso rocks side to side with the music, and he sings along. Mark sticks his sweaty palm out the window to cool it and feels the heat rising up from the asphalt. A gritty wind seems as if it could sandblast the hair off his arm. Adil shouts over the din and points at dervishes of sand dancing along the ridge. A devilish smile crosses his face as he stomps on the pedal, sending the car in a flying leap over the crest of the hill. Their bodies bounce off the seat, hang a moment in the air before slamming back against the upholstery as the tires rejoin the pavement.

They descend the steep grade on the other side, but a sudden letting up on the gas jerks them forward. Adil reaches over, squeezes Mark's leg, and points with his chin at the view opening up before them. The dusty sky is a constantly changing palette of red-spectrum hues over an endless sea of sand dunes. And there, at the bottom of the hill, is a gas station, a blemish on the flesh-colored sands.

Mark still feels the ghost of Adil's hand on his leg though it is back on the wheel. Men in the Middle East touch other men freely. He doesn't know what it means, though he's used to it now after several months in the country. The first time it happened shook him. A few students wanted a picture with their new teacher. One of them threw his arm over Mark's shoulders and leaned in close so that their heads were almost touching, allowing him to detect the scented soap the boy had used mixed with the musty smell of his uniform due for a cleaning.

Before the boy loosened his grip, he gave Mark a brief squeeze. If an officer had walked in the classroom at that moment, Mark would have been reprimanded for the photo, the familiarity, an activity that was not on the program though it lasted only a moment.

They reach the station, a cinder block structure with unfinished outer walls and two old pumps on a dusty lot like a last-chance Texaco you might see on a bend in the road in west Texas. But here the pitiable filling station sits atop vast wealth, deep in the earth, a vast honeycomb of spongy limestone unique to Ash Sharqiyah, the Eastern Province of Saudi Arabia where black crude gushes through the rock. The wealth brings a host of workers like Mark and Adil to the Kingdom.

"Why you laugh?" Adil says.

"Nothing. Are we going to stop?"

He jerks the wheel of the Nissan to the right, cutting in front of a Mercedes so loaded with passengers that its chassis nearly touches the ground. They roar along the narrow side road and pass a line of late-model European and oversized American cars waiting to buy gas. The car skids to a halt in the gravel next to the grit-splattered phone booth at the edge of the lot. As the cloud of dust settles, Adil breaks into laughter. A Michael Jackson tape is now in the player and "Billie Jean" blares from the speakers, causing everyone on the lot to gawk at the intruders and their Western music

After a brief stare, the Saudis return to their families, the men sitting in the front seats, alternately gesticulating and resting their hands and arms on the shoulders of their fellows as they talk. The women sit in back like covered statues with their black veils hiding every part of them except their hennaed hands. They speak in a high-pitched cackle while bright-eyed, happy children in the latest Oshkosh and Gap fashions crawl over their laps.

Some of the men begin to shout at the slow-moving gas attendant, but the small leathery-skinned man ignores their jeers as he shuffles back and forth from one side of the pumps to the other. He wipes his hands on the front of his grease-stained *thobe*, a shirt-like garment hanging down to his ankles, and stares at his two companions who sit nearby. They smoke cigarettes and drink Pepsis while watching a TV resting on a crate, the long extension cord snaking into the cinder block hut. The attendant gazes at the screen and tilts his head as if he senses something, a far-off murmur just beginning.

Adil pulls out a coin purse. "Why you don't get us some Pepsis?"

Mark jumps from the truck and shakes out his legs. "I got it," he says, ignoring the coins Adil rattles in his hand as if he's about to throw dice.

"Okay, my friend." He smiles and his head jerks back, showing the laugh lines on his tan face. Mark has a feeling they are about the same age, but the Pakistani has lived a lot more. He took the contract to teach in Saudi to feed a hunger for more adventure in his life. And now he feels it all around him. He is about as far from his small Midwestern hometown as he can get, and Adil's face is taking him even farther.

He finds the soft drink machine inside the station. Through the dirty window he watches Adil sit back in the car, pulling on the dark, thick hair of his moustache. Then he runs his fingers through his bushy hair, finishing the swept-back style the wind has started.

The outside lights sputter on as Mark comes out of the station, and he hears, "*Allahu Akbar, Allahu Akbar*, God is great," the opening of the Maghreb prayer call. The closest mosque must be miles away. The unnatural brilliance of the TV catches his eye, and he watches images of Saudis in long robes move across the screen, forming into lines on a plush oriental carpet in a marble hall. "*Ashhadu an la illallah*. I bear witness that there is no god but Allah."

The two men watching TV get up, snub out their cigarettes, and walk over to a stainless steel water container that stands on the side of the rough building. The man who has been pumping gas abandons his customers and joins his friends. The three kick off their sandals and wash their feet, splash water on their faces, before proceeding to a small area, sectioned off by a low wall of cinder blocks on the west side of the structure. They stand in a row on a worn rug, raise their hands to their ears, and fall to their knees.

Several of the cars at the pumps pull out of line and get back on the road, unwilling to wait the twenty-five minutes before they can get gas again. Some of the men get out and join their fellow Moslems praying toward Mecca. Not Adil. Mark looks at him and he shakes his head. The voice calls out from the TV and the wail fans out over the dusty remote gas station and then across the desert, connecting with the other callers, forming a blanket of security over the nation.

They don't want to sit in the car and drink the soda while people are praying a few feet away. Adil, with a slight hunch of his shoulders, turns down the music out of respect. "Come on. We go. I must get back to Jubail."

"Is there something special about the Pepsis from this station?"

"What you mean?"

"It was a long drive, I mean, for this." He holds up his nearly empty bottle.

Adil laughs and steps on the gas. "It's the journey, my friend. The journey."

The worn tires kick up tiny stones, creating another cloud of dust. The music blasts as Adil pushes the car into the darkness. No moon or stars. He pulls into the left lane and passes one, two, three cars before the lights of an oncoming truck bear down on them. Mark looks over at the vehicle beside them and sees what he thinks will be his last sight on earth—a camel riding in the back of a Toyota pick-up truck, its thin legs curled under its heavy body and its nose in the air enjoying the night wind. Adil squeezes the car back in line, avoiding a head-on collision by mere seconds. Mark leans back and tries to look unimpressed.

Adil drops him at the front gate of the base. They shake hands, but Adil holds on while he talks, a warm relaxed grip, even rubbing his thumb gently along Mark's thumb. "Next Friday we meet at the coffee place 11:30."

"But... "

"What? You have something else to do?"

"No, but..."

"Okay, see you then." He lets go of his hand. "Goodbye, my friend."

★

Mark leaves his quarters at a bad time. He has a room in a boxy three-story building that looks like a college dormitory on the part of the base where single instructors are housed. Across the way are bungalows with lawns for married men and their wives and children. His ears perk up to the rumble of a small truck and the motor that spews out a cloud of DDT, which wafts over sand-colored boxes with curtained windows, settling on an alien grass that fights the good fight with the sand, brushing like a furtive kiss the petals of flowering oleanders. Normally he would turn around, go back inside, and close the windows until it passes. But he doesn't have time. Adil is supposed to pick him up in a few minutes at the gate.

They've had a weekly rendezvous for a month now, but this time Adil is taking him to Jubail to see where he lives. He passes through the gate and waves to the guard in the gatehouse who knows more about him than he would like, how many times he's been picked up by a non-Saudi in a white Nissan, and perhaps has recorded the license number.

It's sunny and there is no shade. Another man-made cloud smelling of ammonia sails over from the fertilizer plant, burns his nostrils, but neither the odor nor the mosquito control poison hinder the flies that buzz around him. He should have known Adil would be late. He always is.

Only a half hour after the agreed upon time, Adil screeches to a halt outside the gate, waking up the guard who has dozed off. The guard stares at Mark with sleepy eyes, and with his arms crossed on his belly, he nods his chin toward the car as if Mark might not notice his ride has shown up, as if there is no cloud of dust dancing on the air. Mark slows his approach to the car, acting as casual as he can, projecting indifference, beating down the excitement he feels at their weekend away.

In the car Adil shakes his hand and touches his heart. "I pick up two friends from my village. They go with us." In silence they drive the short distance to Dammam and stop at a compound in the industrial area. His friends work at a pipe factory.

They enter a building about the size of Mark's, but where four men live in a room smaller than his. The hall is lined with worn shoes and sandals, some haphazardly kicked off, others neatly matched. Mark has a moment of panic that someone might steal his if he leaves them outside the room. He realizes he's being ridiculous.

A thin, bespectacled man sitting on a single bed with his back against the wall puts the Qur'an aside, stands up to greet them, smiles warmly. Adil's two friends sit shoulder to shoulder on the opposite bed, both small and dark-skinned, identical haircuts, one in a rose-colored *shalwar kameez* and the other in a brown one. They jump up and kiss Adil on both cheeks. They speak almost no English and Mark can't get their names right. "Just call them Ash and Az," says Adil. Ash looks at Mark with dark questioning eyes and makes a hand gesture for eating. Mark shakes his head, but Ash rushes out of the room and slaps down the hall in his sandals. Adil tells him it is custom that guests can't leave a house without having something to eat. In a few minutes he comes back with apples and under-ripe bananas. After the brief repast, they say goodbye to the man who has returned to reading the Qur'an and get on the road.

After a few minutes on the road, they hear the call to pray, and Ash and Az insist they must pray, though Adil tries to talk them out of it. They stop at a mosque made of large white pipes pointing to the sky and cut on an angle at the top like organ pipes. The dome is constructed of shiny green panels, creating an overall effect of hi-tech simplicity. Adil and Mark sit in the car by a large murky puddle and listen to a Bette Midler tape Mark gave him. When Ash and Az crawl into the back seat after their holy experience, they are blasted by the Divine Miss M. at full volume. All the way to Jubail, it is high volume and high speed, zipping past the massive desalination plant.

They come up over a rise and Jubail spreads out in front of them, an endless patchwork of factories and living quarters. The sky has turned so dark with angry clouds the lights have come on, yellow, green, and tiny flashing red ones on the tops of towers scraping the sky. Adil points out Camp 4 where he lives, a large plot of identical prefab boxes arranged without trees or vegetation on streets named Avenue A, B, C, etc. Lightning flashes across the sky, brewing up a new storm.

Adil's three-bedroom, two-bath unit is filthy, the carpet littered with the debris of young single men living together. Empty soda cans are everywhere, and the coffee table is thick with crud. Adil takes Mark's arm. "Okay. We go to play some games at center."

After a couple rounds of pool, the patter of rain starts to beat on the roof. They leave the recreation center and scurry to the car in a raging storm. On the drive back to Camp 4, Mother Nature performs—thunder, lightning and a fierce wind blowing a ready-mix of sand and rain across the road. As Bette wails, Adil drives through a giant puddle spraying water like a fountain, and then turns around to drive through it again, howling with laughter.

★

They lie in bed on their backs.

"Are you sleepy?" Mark says.

"No, are you?"

"Not really." Silence. "Are you going to sleep?"

"I think you don't want to sleep."

"No, just thinking."

"About what?"

"Nothing really. You?" Mark is sure Adil doesn't want to be in bed with a man. Mark's hand brushes Adil's crotch. He's not hard. A hundred times Adil has used the word friend. Can two so different people be friends, in this artificial world, this two-dimensional plane?

"Lock the door," Adil says. Why doesn't he lock the door? It's his room. Putting responsibility on the guest. It's dark. Mark wonders how the lock works. Everything's unfamiliar. Both far from home. If they do it, will they still be friends? Were they ever friends? Do they become something else, something the Pakistani has no word for, or no word he wants to use. And yet weeks of buildup, each one assumes the other wants this. They are men, not boys, but with the uncertainty of boys on another planet without mothers, fathers, brothers, sisters to remind them who they are, or society or the religion they were both brought up with but abandoned.

"Did you lock the door?"

"Yes, I think. I heard a click."

A faint glow from the high window highlights Adil's fear, something Mark has not seen a hint of in the last few weeks. Adil, gregarious. Adil, bold.

Mark knows he will have to go down on him to get things rolling and resents it. His fantasy (seldom realized) is for sex to be two rivers flowing into each other, not a plunge over a waterfall unknowing how the other will react. They are neither drunks nor children to be protected by God. They are men with mustaches, with sweaty bodies in tank tops and underwear, giving off smells of soap harsh and sweet, breath from a pungent dinner not quite suppressed by toothpaste, the angst coming out of pores, the remnants of Pepsi in a glass by the bed, a potpourri of industrial chemicals drifting in the window on sea air. Adil asks again about locking the door.

"Yes. Don't you remember?"

He puts his hand behind Mark's head, directing it toward his pleasure, even though Mark wants to play with the hair on his chest, to lick his hairy tummy first. No time for that.

It is clumsy getting out of their clothes, fitting the condom, the semi-hard penetration and it's over hastily. Adil has a silent orgasm, says he feels the satisfaction and wants to sleep. Mark stares at the shadows on the ceiling.

Morning brings awkwardness. Mark awakes to the groan of a motorbike and rises out of bed. He wanders around the apartment, which looks drearier in the daylight, nothing on the walls except stains. Ash and Az are in the kitchen. They don't seem as friendly, but they serve him tea, terribly sweet Saudi pastries, and spicy party mix left over from the night before. Mark is crazy to leave and go back to his compound, but he doesn't know where to catch a bus and he can't ask the two Pakistanis.

After an hour of Ash and Az trying out their four words of English followed by giggling, Adil stumbles into the kitchen as if he has a hangover, which, of course is impossible in the Kingdom without alcohol. Officially. Mark has wine aging in his closet that he made from grape juice, yeast, and sugar he got at Safeway. The last time he tasted it he nearly barfed. They tell him it gets better after a few months. A little better.

"Good morning," says Adil. "I make some food, and then we go. Okay, my friend?" He lays a hand on Mark's shoulder.

Adil whips up a chicken *kahari* with tomatoes and onions. They eat it with rice and *naan.* It's surprisingly good. They leave the dirty dishes and jump in the car. "Sorry the hurry. I must be back here to receive a call from my mother this afternoon."

After a few miles, the car sputters and dies. They can't restart it. They walk in the brutal heat for twenty minutes to the closest gas station. At the bus stop across the road, Adil tells the bus driver his friends are going to Dammam and the American is going to Al Khobar. He tells Mark he'll call him later.

★

Mark wakes up when someone knocks on his door, announcing he has a call on the hall phone. It's afternoon nap time, when nothing happens except the heat. He flip flops down the dim and empty corridor to the phone. After a quick greeting, Adil says he has something important he wants to talk to Mark about. They agree to meet at the coffee shop in Al Khobar in an hour.

At the entrance to the shopping center, Adil greets Mark with his usual bluster, but something is off, his eyes darting, and his shoulders pulled in taut a fraction of an inch. He waits until several shoppers pass. "My friend, my friend, so happy to see you. I think you miss me after last weekend." His eyebrows make a brief crack at innuendo. Mark remains wooden, causing Adil to pull at his chest hair. Mark continues staring at him, waiting.

"Is everything okay?" Mark says after the next group of shoppers whisk past them and enter the center.

"Oh yeah, of course. Except my car is died. Mechanic fix for temporary, but no good. I have news though. My friend is selling his car, a good one. Only one problem." Mark knows what's coming. Adil changes to pulling on his mustache. Eyes bouncing around like pinballs. "I need help, but only until next paycheck. Two weeks."

Mark smiles. What else can he do when things play out without surprises? "How much help do you need?"

"Let's go in. I buy you a coffee."

Mark waits at the table while Adil gets the drinks. He's steeling himself to say no, thinking of excuses, but does he need an excuse? Loans are bad ideas. Mark has always believed that, especially with someone you've recently had sex with, especially if that person doesn't appear to be a person who normally has sex with men, especially if, as it now seems, that person had a motive, especially if that person is from a completely different culture and might not be bound by the same rules of lending money. All he has to say is one little word. No.

Adil sits down. "Why such a face, my friend? You know you can trust me. I need only five hundred dollars. Is like you think I'm going to ask for thousands. Ha ha ha. No, of course not. This small loan is not so much for you, right?"

Not fair, Mark thinks, for him to play the rich man/poor man card though he does have a point. It's a small fraction of the money he has already saved. If Adil takes time to pay it back, it's no big deal. With each sip of coffee his resolve slips further. "When do you need it?"

"Sorry, can it be tomorrow? Or even if you can go to the bank today. My friend with the car can't wait." He points to a bank on the other side of the foyer from the coffee shop. "Is your bank, no?" Adil knows it is since Mark stopped in one day to make a withdrawal when they were together.

From where he's sitting Mark can see the bank, the teller at the window in a white thobe and red and white ghutrah on his head. No line. He hates the waves inside him, the feeling of being used crashing against the rocks of his privilege as a Westerner.

Adil is playing with his spoon, turning it over and over. His eyes deliberately follow a young Western woman wearing a long skirt and a scarf covering her head. She glances at him and then briskly away. His stare does not stop, focused, his head rotating as naturally as the earth on its axis while she makes her way around the café and down one of the aisles.

Mark stands up with such haste his plastic chair falls over backward, causing a clack that echoes through the center. Adil's stare is broken, his face changes to confusion, and then a smile. Mark picks up the chair. "I'll be right back." He walks toward the bank.

Adil gives Mark a ride back to the base. The car sounds like it will barely make it. Mark gazes at the five hundred dollars showing a slight bulge in the pocket of Adil's tunic. He relaxes about helping his friend. At the gate, Adil offers to drive onto the base, which is allowed if he leaves his ID with the guard. "I can come to your room and thank you properly," he says with his hand on his crotch. Mark emits a phony laugh, lays a hand on Adil's leg. "You should take the money to your friend. Maybe you can come back tomorrow with your new car."

Adil calls the next day to say he won't be able to come by. The following weekend, same story except no call of explanation. Mark goes through the various stages of realization: imagining excuses, wondering if he has offended Adil in some way, applying logic to an otherwise illogical situation, and finally allowing the encroaching voice in his head to tell him he's been had. He keeps backtracking on the final conclusion, unwilling to accept it, not wanting that feeling of being small, weak, a part of him holding out for another explanation.

Mark leans against the cool tiled wall and dials the number. Adil's roommate who speaks a little English answers.

"Can I speak to Adil? This is Mark."

"Yes, Mark. I remember. American friend. Sorry. Adil not here no more."

"What do you mean?"

"He go to Pakistan. He get married."

"Oh. Is he coming back to Saudi Arabia?"

"No way, man."

"But what about the new car he bought?"

"No new car. You want to leave message. Maybe he call here."

"Yeah. Tell him thanks for screwing me over."

"Sorry. I no understand."

"Forget it. No. No message."

"Maybe I come to visit you someday."

"What? Hah. No, I don't think so. Goodbye."

Mark hangs up the hall phone and begins to laugh. A loud hollow laugh. He can't control it as he stumbles down the hall. He gasps and laughs more. A door opens and one of his neighbors looks at him oddly. He gets to his room, pushes the door open, and falls on his bed, still shaking with laughter.

# Shelter in Place

The narrow alleys of the Gothic Quarter pressed in, filling Calvin with the same sense of mystery that would overtake him when he used to venture into the deep woods behind his family house in Indiana. As a boy he imagined wild animals and forest gremlins emerging from the wall of tall trees on either side of the path, though the most dangerous thing that had happened was getting stung by a bee or drenched by a sudden storm. The dark forest of Barcelona's ancient buildings proved a bit more foreboding. A couple months after his arrival in the city on a one-year contract to teach English, he had been dragged into a doorway by a pair of good-looking thugs and relieved of his watch, phone, and wallet. He only blamed himself. He had been warned. It didn't take this small-town boy long to get his street smarts, shake off his corn-fed vulnerability, and once again penetrate the shadowy streets of his newfound city that continually teased him with its secrets.

Years after his innocent days of finding his footing in the city, the old quarter still held a fascination for him despite the quick-time march toward gentrification and resulting loss of its edge. Even El Born, the neighborhood of his robbery, had been tamed from an area of drugs and crime to one of the trendiest parts of the city. What remained unchanged were the stones and bricks of the weathered buildings, which still bled an age-old mist, an essence of bygone days in the air of narrow streets never kissed by the sun, making them bone chilling in the winter and pleasingly cool in the summer.

Calvin passed the cathedral and came to one of the remaining sections of the Roman wall. He chuckled at how differently he saw it now in comparison with those early days when it was simply an ugly patchwork of old stones of varying sizes and colors, particularly the places red brick had been used to repair the crumbling sections. Nigel had educated him about the wall, as he had about so many things, making him see it not as a sloppy patch job, but a multi-textured fabric on which the history of Barcelona was told, the medieval on top of Roman, forming foundations for palaces, churches, and buildings of all styles.

"Go ahead. Touch one of those large gray stones near the base," Nigel had said with a playful smile. "Imagine you are touching a block put in place by workers nearly two thousand years ago, hands that participated in who knows what kind of unmentionable things at night in the work camps."

Calvin swiftly withdrew his hand and gave Nigel a sideways glance. "Really, Nigel."

Nigel laughed, and then launched into a smoker's cough. He took out a pack of Ducados and lit one.

His memory was from the day Nigel had taken him on a tour of the remaining sections of the fourth century wall, filling Calvin's head with dates and details he would never remember. But he couldn't forget the way Nigel had enriched his point of view. Now, lamentably, they no longer spoke. It had been over a year. And yet, each time he passed a part of the wall since their falling out, he imagined going to Nigel's and apologizing. Today was no different, except it was. It was the anniversary of his father's death. That other falling out, which had begun when he was a teenager, was never resolved, not even with his mother working hard to make it so. He didn't arrive back in his hometown in time to say goodbye. He had to live with the failing for the rest of his life. In the case of Nigel, all he had to do was cross Via Laietana into the Sant Pere neighborhood and walk a few blocks to Nigel's house. In these ten years outside the United States, he had learned at least a few of the lessons put before him. It was time to reconnect with Nigel.

At the entrance to Nigel's street, two policemen stood. About halfway down, an ambulance filled the street with its bulky and ominous presence, the red light bouncing off the walls. Calvin nodded to the policemen and attempted to walk past. One of them put out his arm and told him in Catalan the street was blocked off.

"*Mi amigo vive ahi.*" My friend lives there. The ambulance was parked right in front of Nigel's door.

The policeman switched to English. "Is not possible to pass."

At the same moment, two medics wheeled a person out of the building on a stretcher. They wore plastic gear over their faces, nitrile gloves, and disposable coveralls. Because of the oxygen mask over the person's face, it was difficult to see who it was, but his sinking gut told him it was Nigel.

"I think that's my friend," said Calvin. "I need to see him."

The policeman shook his head.

"Can you at least tell me what hospital they are going to?"

"*Hospital Clínic, penso.*"

★

In the early days when Calvin was still a neophyte in the city, he strutted through the Sant Pere neighborhood with calculated sexiness in a tank top, shorts, and flip-flops on his way to meet his friends at Barceloneta Beach. It had only taken him a short time in Barcelona to achieve his goal—a nearly complete break from his Indiana past, acceptance in an international group of hedonistic friends, and more sex than he ever imagined possible. With each new day he learned to communicate better in Spanish. He renewed his contract at the Institute, which provided him with the disposable income to buy new clothes and to travel, and he had already gone on several sex holidays to hotspots in Spain and Morocco.

He stopped to look at a pair of sneakers in the window of one of the many boutiques that had sprung up in the area. In the building next door, shutters creaked open, and an older man peered out from behind the bars with the desolate expression of a man in prison. Calvin glanced at him and seeing he was of a certain age, rapidly unsaw him and returned to the shoes.

"I say, there. Do you speak English?"

For a moment, Calvin pretended he didn't hear or didn't understand. The sneakers were high tops and a lovely shade of powder blue. Looked to be about his size. Could he afford them? They would look so cool with the tight jeans he had bought the week before. He twitched and sensed a cracking under the pressure of the man's waiting eyes. After all, he was a Midwesterner and had been brought up properly. He sighed and turned toward the man. "I do."

"I wonder if you would be so kind as to do me a favor. I'm in a bit of a bind. You see, I'm a little under the weather and I need a prescription picked up. The pharmacy is just at the corner." He tilted his head and raised his eyebrows in question. His rheumy eyes pleaded.

Poor guy, old, sick, and British. Calvin felt sorry for him on three accounts. He hadn't completely lost empathy for humans outside of his peer group, though he didn't necessarily want to interact with them if he didn't have to. He hesitated.

"I'm sorry. I shouldn't have asked."

"No, no problem. I can do it."

"You're a lifesaver." He handed Calvin a scrap of paper through the bars with his name and prescription number on it and pointed to the pharmacy up the block.

Calvin headed at a swift pace to the corner, feeling annoyed, and then annoyed at his annoyance, ultimately conceding how ridiculous he was being. It was a simple favor. His friends could wait a few minutes. His irritation returned when he entered the pharmacy and saw a line. And then the cashier insisted on speaking Catalan to him even when he answered in Castilian Spanish.

He hurried back to the window from which the man had beckoned him, but he was gone and the interior shutters closed. He found what he imagined to be the correct door and lifted the tarnished brass knocker. As he cursed under his breath, he knocked several more times.

The man opened the door in the same paisley bathrobe and slippers, but he looked slightly more put together with his hair combed. Calvin handed him the bag.

"Please come in."

"I can't. I'm meeting some friends."

"Oh come, come, now. You young people are always in such a hurry. Let me fix you some tea." He produced a devilish grin. "Or something a bit stronger for your trouble?"

Behind the man a polished wooden stairway lined with tapestries led up to the second floor living quarters. At the top an antique table held a large ceramic vase filled with fresh flowers. Calvin had often fantasized living in an apartment in the old quarter, but had never seen the inside of one. He didn't know when he might have the opportunity again. "I guess I could come in for a minute."

"Brilliant." The man bowed and waved Calvin in. "Welcome to my humble abode."

Calvin followed the man up the stairs, feeling underdressed, his flip-flops slapping against the wood and breaking the museum-like serenity of the house. At the top of the stairs, the man ushered him into a living room of brocade-covered antiques and oriental carpets, floor-to-ceiling bookcases, and framed paintings. He went to a side table with several bottles of liquor on it.

"How about some rum? I brought this back from Cuba last month." He pointed at the label. *"Añejo."*

"What does that mean?"

"Aged. Seven years." He walked over to show Calvin the bottle with an increased color in his cheeks. "It goes down quite smooth."

"I'll try a little."

"I'm Nigel, by the way. I'd shake your hand, but I've had a little cold and I don't want you to catch anything."

"Calvin. Nice to meet you."

"The pleasure is all mine." He poured two fingers of rum into a low glass and handed it to him.

Calvin sipped the rum while Nigel gave him a tour of his home with the excitement of a boy showing off his Christmas gifts. Nigel's eyes occasionally lingered too long on the young man's face, making Calvin uncomfortable. They returned to the living room, and he downed the rest of his drink. He set the glass on the coffee table.

"Thank you for showing me your home, but I really have to go."

Nigel's face seemed to age in seconds, his disappointment collapsing his shoulders. But as a few more seconds ticked by, he fashioned a stiff upper lip and produced a business card from the pocket of his robe. "Lovely to meet you."

Calvin stared at the card. Nigel Anthony Saxton III.

"I would be delighted if you stopped by again. I promise not to send you on any more errands."

Calvin stuck the card in his wallet, imagining he would soon dispose of it, and hurried out the door, not looking back though he felt the man staring after him.

He didn't mention his strange encounter with Nigel to his beach friends even though the warm buzz from the rum kept flashing him back to the meeting. But after a few beers, dips in the sea, cruising stares from passersby, and the usual campy banter, Calvin soon forgot about Nigel. Calvin and his friends stayed until sunset, went home to change and shower, and met up for a late dinner before heading to the disco where he hooked up with a young Italian with ridiculously long eyelashes. The order of his life was restored.

A brisk fall breeze swept down La Rambla though the sun shone bright. Calvin stopped at one of the bird seller stalls in front of the Hotel Rivoli Rambla. Hundreds of caged birds filled the air with chirping, and made Calvin think of the sky blue parakeet named Dickie he'd trained as a kid to say a few words. It brought up the usual feelings of regret when he remembered how his father had taken an interest in the bird even when his own had waned. His father was visibly saddened when Dickie keeled over one day.

He was brought back from his reverie by someone calling out, "Calvin." He turned toward the voice and recognized the man, but had forgotten his name. It had been several weeks. "Oh, hello."

The gentleman removed his sunglasses. "You were kind enough to pick up my prescription from the pharmacy. I'm Nigel if you don't remember."

"Yes, I remember. How are you feeling?"

"Tip top. How kind of you to ask. Are you thinking of a bird?"

"I had a parakeet growing up. Taught it to say a few words."

"Like what?"

"Pretty bird and give me a kiss. Then it would make a kissing noise."

"Sounds lovely. You must have had a far nicer childhood than mine."

"For a while...until it wasn't."

Nigel opened his mouth as if to pursue the topic, and then stopped. "Which way are you walking?"

"Toward Columbus." At the end of La Rambla was a statue of Christopher Columbus on a tall pedestal that rose above the harbor.

"Going that way myself. You know, people assume he is pointing toward the new world, your world," he chuckled. "But his finger isn't actually indicating that way at all. It's now generally believed he's oriented to simply point out to sea."

Nigel brought up trivia about any number of things on their walk, details that Calvin had missed in his many *paseos* down La Rambla, always too busy looking at people, or more precisely, men.

When they arrived at the large, sunny plaza of the Columbus monument, Calvin gazed upward and shielded his eyes to verify the direction of the pointing finger while Nigel explained the various griffins, other historical figures, and medallions decorating the base of the statue. Calvin, already in a listless mood, was left catatonic by the sheer amount of information and the professor-like drone of Nigel's voice. So when Nigel suggested they go have lunch in a cozy little place behind La Boqueria, he found it easier to nod yes than to make excuses.

Prompted by his discomfort at sitting across the table from someone people might think was his sugar daddy, Calvin internally scoffed at Nigel's hideous choice of attire, a brown velvet jacket with an orange scarf thrown over his shoulder. After the second cocktail, he loosened up and laughed at Nigel's often-hilarious accounts of his travels. He also noted Nigel spoke fluent Spanish to the waiter.

"I'm surprised your Spanish is so good," said Calvin.

"Why do you say that?"

"I just figured that since you reached out to me on the street that day, you were hesitant to ask a favor of a Spanish speaker."

An amused smile took charge of Nigel's lips under a pencil moustache, another aspect of his appearance Calvin found absurd. "I confess. You caught my attention as the brightest thing to enter my dark street in a fortnight. You positively glowed in a ray of sunlight that trickled down through the balconies and cornices. It was providence."

"Oh," said Calvin with a gulp. A game had been launched, and he had absolutely no desire to be a player.

"My goodness," Nigel said with a laugh and hand on his chin. "I'm afraid I've bowled you over. Don't worry, my boy. I assure you, you're perfectly safe with me." He laughed again.

When the check came, Nigel grabbed it while Calvin pulled out his wallet and removed a couple of bills. Nigel shook his head and shooed away Calvin's money.

"Please," Calvin said rather unconvincingly.

"Don't be ridiculous. The one thing my family did for me was leave me a substantial income. Nothing gives me more pleasure than to treat a nice young man to a meal."

Calvin formed a malicious smile. "Do you do that often?"

Nigel guffawed, seemingly pleased he had gotten under Calvin's skin. "No. In fact, it's rather rare, making it all the more pleasant when the occasion arises."

"I'll get the next one," Calvin blurted out, not realizing at first what he was implying.

"By all means."

While walking back up La Rambla, Nigel pointed at the Opera house. "Have you ever been inside the Liceu?"

"Uh, no."

"I have tickets to a ballet next Saturday. I was going to invite my neighbor, Mildred, but she's an insufferable bore. I'd much prefer to go with you if you're willing."

"Ballet is not my thing. Thank you, though."

"Are you sure? The ballet is wonderful, particularly if you're as enthralled with men's bodies as I suspect you are."

"That's making assumptions."

"My dear boy, it's quite easy to see whose team one plays for when you follow a young man's eyes and see upon which sex they land."

"Okay, Sherlock, but I'm not interested in watching a bunch of men prance around on a stage. I don't care how developed their bodies are."

Nigel's face hardened and his eyes narrowed. "Barcelona has a lot more to offer than partying, pounding disco music, and multiple sex partners."

"There you go again with your assumptions. You don't know me or what my life is like. In any case, what makes you think I would want to hang out with the likes of you? I have plenty of friends." Calvin stormed off and entered the Liceu metro station, mumbling to himself.

When Calvin got home, he slammed the apartment door, letting everyone in the building know his anger. Janet, his roommate, was in the living room reading a book and nearly jumped out of her chair.

"Sorry," said Calvin.

"What's wrong? Some hot number cancel a date?"

"Ha ha." Janet was a colleague at the Institute and the sister he never had. He proceeded to tell her the story of Nigel.

"Sounds like you let him get to you."

"No way. He's a silly old queen. They're all after the same thing."

"Hmm. Maybe he's got a point."

"No. Don't do that. Judgmental is not your thing."

"Calvin, you go out five nights a week, get drunk, and drag home countless tricks. Barcelona *does* have a lot more to offer."

"I can find another apartment if you like."

"Don't be an ass. I'm just saying maybe this guy can show you a part of the city you wouldn't see on your own."

Calvin stayed home that night to prove everyone wrong. He slept poorly. In the morning he found the card still in his wallet, called Nigel, and agreed to go to the ballet. Over the next few years, they went to museums, concerts, and dinners in undiscovered restaurants in out-of-the way corners of the city. Occasionally Calvin insisted on paying. He still had his nights out with the boys, his nameless one-night stands, and his Sunday mornings sleeping until noon. On their occasional evening out, Nigel was a perfect gentleman, and they would shake hands at the end of the night. Janet was the only friend who was aware of these secret adventures.

When Calvin received word his father had a heart attack, he went to Nigel for advice.

"He was such an asshole when he found out I was gay. He threw me out of the house. I said I would never speak to him again."

"You have to go," said Nigel. "Don't make him go to his grave with the burden of alienating his son. Be the bigger man. Forgive him."

Calvin booked a flight for the next day. His mother called that night saying his father had passed. The pain of his father's death and the unresolved nature of their quarrel rattled him. He had gone to Nigel in his time of crisis, and Nigel, roughly his father's age, took on a larger role as someone he trusted, someone to ask for advice.

At the Hospital Clínic emergency desk, Calvin found out little except a confirmation Nigel had been admitted. They wouldn't let him see him.

"Are you family?" The woman's lined face and tired eyes showed the signs of being overwhelmed. The phone kept ringing and people behind Calvin shouted questions about loved ones.

"I'm a friend. He doesn't have any family here."

She sighed. "Don't know why I asked. Force of habit. They wouldn't let you see him even if you were family."

"Why's that?"

"He's been isolated in a special ICU unit. Check back tomorrow. We'll know more."

Calvin went back to Nigel's building and rang Mildred's apartment. After saying his name on the intercom, several long, silent moments passed before the buzzer sounded to let him in. She stood at the door, shoulders drooping and a palette of negative emotions on her face: pale worry about Nigel mixed with a narrow-eyed suspicion of Calvin. She had been Nigel's companion before Calvin came along, his date for concerts, museum tours, and dinners out. When Nigel extended his first invitation to go to the ballet, he had described Mildred as an insufferable bore, though Calvin later learned it was merely an excuse to make his invitation seem less weighty. The three of them had twice gone out to eat where Calvin learned she had worked at the Institute but retired before Calvin began his contract. She filled him in about the history when business boomed, salaries and benefits were high, before the big strike and shakeup.

"Earlier I came to see Nigel, but there was an ambulance." He was out of breath and cowered under her skeptical gaze. "I went to the Hospital Clínic. They wouldn't let me see him."

"I thought you two..."

"I had come to apologize. Everything was my fault.

Has he been sick?"

Her face softened. "Come in. I'll make some tea."

They sat at the kitchen table in awkward silence as Mildred's cat kept brushing up against Calvin's legs.

Mildred poured the tea. "I do hope it's not that corona thing. He's been feeling terrible lately. I hear him coughing at night. The reports from China on the news are terrible. He's at risk, you know, with his history of respiratory illness and those damn cigarettes he smokes."

"It's probably just the flu. Haven't heard of many cases in Spain. I was surprised when they asked me at the hospital if he had family they could call. Of course, I didn't have any information about that. I think he mentioned a sister once."

"They weren't close. I don't think he's spoken to her in years."

"Do you know if he has his phone with him? I need to send him a message."

"I have a key to his apartment. I could look." She stared at Calvin fixedly. "You know, he never told me what happened between you two. It pained him deeply."

"It was stupid, and now it seems especially so. I could have handled it so much better. About a year ago, after a concert at the Palau, I suggested we go to a bar in Eixample. He told me he hadn't been to a gay bar in ages and hated being the granddaddy among all the hottie boys as he called them. I convinced him to go, and I kept telling myself it would be fine. Surely he would enjoy the scenery. The place was full with the pre-disco crowd and the music loud. He was uncomfortable, but I hoped a few drinks would make him more relaxed. We overdid it. We left the place holding each other up and took a taxi back here. I got him into his apartment, and when I tried to leave, he insisted I help him into the bedroom. He pulled me into a hug and kissed my neck, my face. It all happened so fast. I mean, his breath from the Ducados was bad enough. The whole thing made me sick. The more I tried to push him away, the more persistent he became. He declared his love for me. I panicked."

"Oh, come on. You act as if you weren't aware. I knew from the first moment I saw you together."

"Nothing sexual had ever happened. We went for years with nothing more than a handshake. He would occasionally say flirty things, you know, but I always assumed he was joking."

She shook her head. "How blind we are sometimes. So what did you do?"

"I pushed him hard, and he fell back on the bed. I was angry. I stormed out of the apartment. He sent me several texts apologizing. But I still had that horrible feeling in my gut, a tingly kind of betrayal he had been lying to me all along by pretending he only wanted my companionship. I never wanted to be in that position again."

"And how do you think he felt? He must have been devastated."

"I know. I was selfish, only thinking of me. It took a while, but I eventually crawled out of my cave and got angry with myself for being so blind, for handling the situation so badly, acting the victim. By the time the realization of what had happened caught up with me, months had passed. I chose the easy route of doing nothing. But I always had the feeling I would run into him or go to his apartment one day, and ask for his forgiveness. Unfortunately, that day was today."

"I hope you still have that chance to make it right."

"Don't say that. I'm sure he'll be all right." But inside Calvin was worried, and surprised how much he cared.

That night in bed, Calvin remembered how Nigel made him laugh, and little by little, see the world in a different way. He had been forced to look at himself in the mirror and face that his self-indulgent party boy days would have to end one day, and what would be left? Nigel had shown him a sample of the city's many delights. And how had he repaid him? With a petty and selfish rebuff to Nigel's desperate attempt to express his love.

Ten days later, the city was on lockdown, some of the most social, out-in-the-street people on earth confined to their homes. Nigel was still in the ICU in critical condition and Mildred had passed by the hospital to drop off his phone. Calvin sent him numerous video messages he had been able to record before the lockdown in front of places they had been together like the Roman wall or the Columbus monument or the Palau de la Música. Nigel would respond with a thumbs up or happy face emoji, apparently all he had the energy for. Calvin took it as a sign Nigel forgave him. But even those minimal responses ceased. A few days later, Mildred called to say he had passed during the night. Her voice was so fragile it sounded as if it might shatter into a thousand pieces. Calvin assumed it was because of her grief. And then she told him she had been ill. Her doctor had ordered the test, and she was going in the next day.

Under gray skies and a light rain, the people of Calvin's barrio and all over the city stepped out on their balconies clapping and banging pots in what had become a nightly ritual, sending out a message of support for doctors, nurses, and medical personnel on the front lines of the battle. Calvin ferociously beat an old metal pan long after his neighbors had stopped, knowing that when he stopped, the tragedy of Nigel and Mildred and the unknown others would overtake him.

As darkness descended over the city, Calvin fell into a plastic chair with the pan and spoon in his lap. The cold metal touched his bare knee and made him shiver. He looked in through the balcony doors at Janet standing at the stove, her back to him, stirring a pot of soup. Would she be next? Would he? How many lives would be lost in this city he had grown to love? How many would not be able to say goodbye or ask forgiveness of friends or loved ones they had wronged?

Across the narrow street, a man sat in his living room, the TV emitting a constantly changing light that turned his face from blue to red to purple. He shifted his gaze toward Calvin with fear in his eyes. He lived alone. He had a blanket around his hunched shoulders despite the warm night.

# Reunion

The sign stood up and punched Adam in the gut with the news he had entered the city limits of his hometown, "The Soybean Capital of the World." He was not surprised the population had declined considerably. And the elevation of a meager six hundred plus feet above sea level was a figure he had forgotten or never knew. Flatland. A land between rivers. He was surrounded by black silty loam you could grow anything in or sink into or get buried in.

It had been fifty years since his post high school exodus, cutting himself off from everything that had sustained him the first eighteen years of his life—Kelly's potato chips, root beer from Elam's, beefsteak tomatoes his grandma grew, and sweet corn from his uncle's farm out by Mt. Zion. Adam Montroy had been corn fed and hand punished by a father who did not believe in sparing the rod. He was a Midwestern boy at heart no matter how much he tried to deny it. And now, having entered the boundaries that had once defined his existence, he couldn't stop the flood of memories, every street sign, every recognized building stirring things up, the very air heavy with moisture and regret.

Boarded up houses slated for destruction lined the wide avenue shuttling traffic from the main highway to the center of town, and on the other side of the street, staring at the empty homes, were shuttered factories, all hard edges and stark landscapes, weeping rust, oxidized tears for the stilted dreams of their workers. Adam peered into the gaping holes of broken windows with the same sinking loss he had experienced when staring into the eyes of former lovers who didn't feel the same anymore.

Red light after red light slowed his progress—brake, clutch, gas, release clutch, over and over—giving Adam plenty of opportunities to turn around, stop this nervous flutter in his heart, and backtrack out of town. He might have done it if he hadn't been so tired of driving, his left leg aching from managing the stick shift Subaru a friend had lent him after flying into Chicago, the clutch requiring muscles not used in recent years and an aging body not wanting to cooperate. Like his hometown, he was descending into a shadow of what he once was. He sought easier paths, took shortcuts and naps, and nothing appealed to him more at that moment than a nap as the afternoon wore down.

At one red light, an odor drifted in the open window, unlike anything he had encountered in his travels around the world. What they as kids had described as a curious mix of vomit and fermented garbage was a by-product of agribusiness, the processing of corn and soybeans at one of the local factories. One thing hadn't changed or gotten worse. It simply was, a force demanding attention, an olfactory pall over the low-lying town. A remembrance bloomed in his head of a biting winter night at a rundown house reeking of bleach and cheap perfume on this same street where ladies offered their services to wayward boys. Along with two drunk friends, he was relieved of his virginity in a blur of awkwardness. When he left the house at two in the morning, he was chased to the car by a particularly bad incidence of the factory smell coupled with the unchangeable fact his first time had been with a prostitute, a woman he did not want.

He stepped on the gas to try to break the chain of red lights, but to no avail. The glowing disc of the traffic light taunted him like an angry emoji. He tapped his fingers on the steering wheel and made an angry face right back at the light. While he waited, he stared at children playing in a yard knee-high with weeds, around them broken glass reflecting the sun, summer beating down on them but not slowing their frantic need for play now that school no longer kept them in its grips.

Crows lined up on the telephone lines, facing the children and whisking the air with their brash cawing. In a town going down, everything and everyone trying to survive, who knew what large hungry birds might do? But the kids were small and scrawny, and one crow shrugged its feathers and took off. The others followed. The light changed. Foot off the brake, foot on the gas, release the clutch, tedious. Just as he got to third gear, a pothole loomed, causing him to swerve and brake, engine coughing. Then stomping on the clutch, he had to start the progression of gears all over again.

The parking lot of the renovated building where he had rented an apartment was conspicuously empty. The location was two blocks from the university, though seemingly miles away as if an imaginary red line had been drawn at the southeast corner of the campus, carving out a neighborhood more Black than white, more poor than rich, a not too subtle reminder for the liberal arts students the world they might withdraw from was at their doorstep.

Adam was in town for his fiftieth high school reunion. He had chosen a short-term rental in order to avoid any embarrassing encounters in the hallways or at breakfast in the hotel where the festivities were to be held and where most of the out-of-town attendees were staying. The offerings on the rental website were slim. He settled on an economically priced one bedroom, which from the pictures appeared staged for an open house. But what most intrigued him about the listing was the host's profile indicating he resided in Bogota. It showed a picture of a young man of dusky charm and innocence, plucking the strings of his foreign lover fantasy, so different from the fair-haired farm boy from Wichita he had married (he did claim to be ten percent Native American, Shawnee to be precise).

Adam's curiosity led him to initiate an online chat over the unlikelihood of a young Colombian managing a building in the heart of the decaying Midwest. Carlos responded with his opinion Decatur was a city with excellent investment opportunities. Adam laughed. He went online and found not only a horrifying picture of the 16-unit brick building pre cosmetic upgrades, but the real estate history. It sold for $250,000 in 2006 and then $150,000 in 2018. You could take the price paid for the sixteen-unit building, multiply it four times, and if you were lucky, buy a one-bedroom apartment in a sketchy neighborhood back home in California. Was this trending? Foreign investors buying up great swaths of the devastated Midwest?

Adam punched in the code and retrieved the key from a lock box attached to the outside of the building. He inserted the key into the lock of the glass and metal front door, and then had to tug on the handle, causing the bottom to scrape the sill with a noise that rattled his frayed nerves. Inside, a row of mailboxes accompanied a row of lock boxes containing keys to the individual apartments. He entered another code to extract the key for his apartment. In short-term rental parlance, it was called a self check-in.

The hallway was cool, quiet, and dimly lit, no signs of life behind the doors on either side. To all appearances it was an abandoned building, which wouldn't surprise him as he had a hard time believing the place would attract many short-term renters in this neighborhood.

In a far-off corner of the building, he heard heavy steps descending from the upper floor. He wanted to duck into his apartment, but he hadn't been able to locate the number before a large man in baggy jeans and a soiled shirt barrelled through a swinging door leading to the back section of the building. He had a cloudy eye and a limp. The man stopped short when he realized another person was in the hall. It was hard to say which of them appeared more startled.

"I'm looking for number ten," said Adam in a tremulous voice.

"Oh, yeah. I heard somebody's checking in today. I'm Charles, maintenance." The drawn-out vowels made the accent nearly Southern, the downstate Illinois manner of speaking Adam had gone to great lengths to eliminate from his speech. "Your apartment is through this here door to the back."

"Am I the only one in the building?"

"Naw. There a nice lady right next to you. She here

for some kind a reunion, high school or something."

"Me, too. Fifty-year reunion. I haven't been back since graduation." Charles stared at him with his one good eye, making Adam uncertain about his lodging choice. Everything about the building was bathed in eerie mystery as if a setup for a horror film.

"You here by yourself? No family or nothing."

"Only me."

"Looks like you and that lady got something in common. She a nice-looking woman." A wry smile sprung on his face like he imagined the two of them hooking up.

He told Adam a little of the building's history, how these two young Spanish guys (he meant Spanish speakers) bought the building and fixed it up. They came by to check on things from time to time. Something about the way he discussed them made Adam think they were a couple.

Inside the apartment, the odor of stale tobacco spilled over him despite the newly painted walls, the new flooring, new furniture, and "no smoking" policy. No amount of layering could cover up the residue deep with the walls. He imagined a pre-makeover resident, a chain smoker, someone out of work, sitting on a ratty sofa watching game shows and measuring the passing of hours with snubbed out cigarettes piling up in an ashtray.

He dropped his bags and fell onto the sofa fully intending to escape into a siesta. But his mind, soaking in the air of his youth, had other ideas. His head buzzed with memories: the piano lessons in the university practice rooms a couple blocks away; the steakhouse nearby where his family used to celebrate birthdays; the thrift store on the same block where he first bought tattered clothes so he could look like a hippie. These were the kinds of memories he and Eloise would laugh about when they spoke by phone. She had been his prom date senior year and was the only person from high school he communicated with.

"I think it'll be good for you to come. You might be surprised," Eloise had said by phone. "Holding shame in your heart for so long is not healthy."

"Nope. Gone. Don't even think about it."

"Liar."

She had gone to each decade reunion and insisted, after each one, on reporting to Adam how much better she was doing than most of the class. She had settled outside Seattle with her second husband and a herd of rescue dogs in a house overlooking Puget Sound. She also reported everyone asked about him, but she had failed to convince him anybody truly cared. When the fifty-year reunion invitation appeared in his mailbox, he accused Eloise of revealing his whereabouts. She maintained it was the relentless self-appointed class historian who had managed to track him down, no easy feat as he had moved no less than twenty times since he left his hometown.

Not long after receiving the invitation, he had thumbed through the mail, mostly junk going directly to the garbage, until he came upon what appeared to be a letter in a store-bought envelope with a USPS stamp, an actual letter from a real person, not one of those promotions made to look personal in a handwriting font. The return address flipped his stomach. Derek Edwards, a name he had not succeeded in erasing from his memory.

Even more reason to toss it. But the nagging voice of curiosity got the better of him and he slid his finger under the flap.

"Dear Adam," the letter began in stylish cursive. He had gotten Adam's address from Eloise. A surge of anger blazed inside him, but he would deal with Eloise later. Derek said he would have written sooner, years ago if he had known where to find him. The notion of forgiveness had been weighing on him since he had reached a point of sufficient strength to let bygones be bygones. He understood the pressure Adam had been under, and if the roles had been reversed, he might have done the same thing. To Adam, it was obvious the roles couldn't have been reversed for the simple reason Adam devoted all his energy back then to appearing straight, to curry favor with the gang even if it meant bowing to bullies. Derek, on the other hand, was soft and kind and unable to control his hands, which often appeared like birds wanting to fly away. Adam used to look at him angrily and wonder why he didn't care if people pegged him as queer. Most of Derek's friends were girls, Eloise one of them.

Adam shuddered at the memory of Cliff's brutal voice resonating in his head. "Come on, Adam, give him a kick. You know you've always wanted to for the way he looks at you."

At the prom, Cliff corralled Adam in the restroom and demanded he invite Derek outside. The subtext screamed somebody was getting a beating that night and if it wasn't Derek, it would be Adam. Adam allowed himself to be bait, luring Derek outside with the promise of beer in his car. They each got a beer from the trunk and Adam pointed toward the bleachers. Despite the shadows or maybe because of them, Derek followed. The others pounced, Cliff, Randy, and Jude. They pushed Derek like a pinball between them, calling him *fag, fairy, queer.* Derek swung his arms and landed a few half-assed punches. They continued to taunt him, saying he fought like a girl. With the boys now warmed up, things took a turn for the worse. They knocked him to the ground face down and Cliff started kicking him.

Anger and fear churned Adam's insides, but if he didn't join in, he would be next. After the first kick, self-loathing gripped his throat, and yet it didn't stop him from connecting two more times with the now defenseless body on the ground. Derek had stopped resisting and curled up in fetal position, arms protecting his head.

When Adam came back into the dance, his clothes were disheveled, and spots of what looked like blood dotted his new suede shoes. Eloise confronted him. "Where's Derek?"

He walked by her in slow motion. The others entered with the look of a fresh kill on their faces. She ran out the door and found Derek, took him to the hospital. She didn't talk to Adam for months, refused his phone calls. The day before he left for college he camped out on her doorstep. He confessed his cowardice.

"It's not me you should be asking for forgiveness," said Eloise

"I can't right now. But I will. I promise."

She didn't believe him, but his pain was obvious, and that was something.

★

Little pockets of older folks stood awkwardly, bathed in the bright, unflattering fluorescent tube lighting with its tiny buzz sounding louder than the hushed chatter of polite conversation. Adam smelled fried chicken as he entered the warehouse-like room in the back of the restaurant, reserved for the gathering, the first event of the reunion. Heads turned and commas fell into sentences. The organizer, a woman Adam did not remember from high school, greeted him by name in a casual lilt as if they had spoken the day before. She stuck out her soft hand and reminded him her name was June.

"I'm Adam," he said despite the fact she had just addressed him so.

She smiled demurely, as if recognizing the uneasiness of it all. "Where's Eloise? I thought you guys were coming together." Fifty years had passed, and yet, in her mind and no doubt many of the classmates, old connections remained strong. People at reunions searched for associations, liked to put people in couples and groups, lean on something familiar.

"She was delayed. Family stuff. I was going to pick her up at her parents' house, but she told me to go ahead."

Across the room a woman screamed. "Adam Montroy!" Sherry sashayed over, her body jiggling with excitement, and her smile expanding like a time-lapse video of a flower blooming. She pulled him into an embrace so violently he nearly lost his balance. While still holding on to him, she pulled out her phone and snapped a selfie. "I'm sending this to Sam right now. Can you believe Eloise, Sam, you and I are going to be in the same room for the first time in fifty years?"

Adam's stomach flipped with the memory of the last time the four of them were together, prom night, their double date, the fearless four becoming the scattered four by the end of the night.

"Eloise better get here soon. Shit. Where is the waitress with the drinks? I'm thirsty," she snorted. Sherry was exactly the same, lovingly brash, full of life, a storm you welcomed. She could tell a dumb joke you'd heard a thousand times and still make you laugh. The next minute she asked Adam why he hadn't brought his partner.

"Husband," Adam corrected. In truth his husband was having an affair and the road to nirvana had recently gotten quite rocky, but he had decided not to share information that might destroy any of the newly found gay romance fantasies among the ladies.

She guffawed. "I know that." And then she launched right into the breaking news of her fifteen-year-old grandson's announcement he had a boyfriend. "I love my grandson to death. Kids these days don't give a shit what people think."

The two women she had been talking to, Gwen and Astrid, inched toward us, waiting to be invited into our orbit. Sherry motioned for Gwen to come closer, reached out, and took her arm. "Gwen's ex finally came out. What a closet case! You don't mind me telling Adam, do you, honey?"

Gwen threw up her hands.

"There she is with the cocktails," said Astrid.

Sherry shrieked again, but not in anticipation of her Long Island Iced Tea. Eloise had just walked in the door.

Adam found himself in the middle of an adoring harem, all attached to his light by revealing how close they were to someone who was gay. They occupied one end of the table and the ladies lobbed questions at him. Everyone was up-to-date on Adam being gay and married to a man named Edward. Eloise clearly was the carrier pigeon, working her revenge in small ways all these years later. Not that anyone seemed to care. At least the women. He wondered if it might have been easier if everyone had treated him like a pariah, allowing him to stomp out, return to his depressing digs, pack his bags, and forget this tremulous notion of righting the past.

The server arrived with a gigantic tray of pre-ordered fried chicken dinners and wiggled between conversations to plop the huge plates in front of them. The chicken glistened with grease and the mashed potatoes looked impossibly smooth and glossy. A man at the other end of the table proclaimed, "Hot damn!" at the sight of the meals. Adam looked to see if it was someone he knew. He didn't recognize a single man at the table, which was a good thing as he wasn't quite ready to face Derek, and certainly not any of his tormentors from back in the dark ages. He wondered if he would recognize them. In the battle of the sexes, the men had clearly lost if the people at the table were any indication. Most of the women looked ten years younger than the men. "I don't see Derek," said Eloise. "I wonder if he got lost."

★

Adam and Eloise sat in the car in the parking lot smoking a joint Eloise described as kick-ass. As the high ramped up, bumping up against the several cocktails, Adam lost track of where they were. His vacant stare fell on the low buildings in front of them, corrugated siding painted mint green with snappy red awnings. He squinted and sounded out the words on the sign, "VFW Post 99."

"Yep," confirmed Eloise.

"No fucking way." The scene had all the elements of a bad dream: dim lighting, distorted vision, a certain distance from reality. "Why?" Adam whined.

"Frank from our class plays guitar in a band doing covers from the 60s, 70s, and 80s."

"And we're lucky enough he happens to be playing tonight. I have no idea who he is."

"Just go with it. Everybody else is already inside."

They opened the door into an alternative universe with the band playing Billy Ray Cyrus's "Achy Breaky Heart." Adam turned around to walk out, but Eloise grabbed his arm. "Buckle up, buttercup."

About twenty people, the majority older than the reunion group, were on the dance floor under a mirrored disco ball, doing a line dance, the men in caps showing their military branch and country of service. The women wore baggy jeans or long skirts, and the ones with platform sandals made Adam fear for their lives. None of the reunion crowd had yet joined the dancers, but had commandeered a large table near the front. Adam and Eloise dashed to the bar and begged the bartender, a man with a long gray ponytail, to make their drinks doubles. Sherry waved them over to the big table, but Eloise pretended she didn't see her and led Adam to a booth where they could finally talk.

"You remember my little brother, Lance, right?"

"Doesn't he live in Montana?"

"He's in Southern California now. Separated. He finally admitted what I've suspected for a long time."

Adam tried to control his eyes from rolling and rallied to act surprised. "No!"

"He won't come out. Can't, he says. It's too late."

"It's never too late."

"I've done my part. Let him know it doesn't matter to me. I only want him to be happy." She knocked back half her drink.

"Coming out doesn't necessarily make you happy."

"I know. But not coming out can make you even more miserable, especially when you've identified, at least to yourself, that little glitch in your life."

"Little glitch?"

"Okay. Not so little. But in the greater scheme of things, is it really important? My brother is exactly the same wonderful person I've always loved."

Their former classmates from the big table got up to dance when the band launched into The Kinks's "You Really Got me." The song jerked both Adam and Eloise back to prom night. They had danced to that song. They glanced at each other, and then away, a curious vibration overtook them like the guitar player was strumming the chords on their nerves. And the little glitch grew significantly larger as Adam remembered how Derek had been perilously close to ending up like Mathew Shepard, the young man who had been beaten, lashed to a prairie fence in Wyoming, and left to die.

Awkwardness pounded at Adam's temples. "Should we join them?"

"You're not digging this conversation?"

"I don't know what to say. He has to make the choice. It can't be forced."

By the time they finished their drinks and joined the dancers, the music had changed, bumping them into the eighties with Michael Jackson's "Thriller." Sherry gave them the stink eye for ignoring her. A few seconds later she abandoned Gwen and Astrid to boogie over to them. "I'm crashing your party whether you like it or not." Her happy face fell into an exaggerated sad one. "I wish Sam were here. He's getting in tomorrow." A couple of years after their prom date, Sherry had married her high school sweetheart. And later divorced him. And then married him again.

Eloise and Sherry proceeded to dance side-by-side, attempting to mimic the zombie dancers of the "Thriller" video. They side-stepped in sync, scrunching their shoulders, flopping their hands, and whipping their heads from left to right.

Adam laughed and tried his own version of a zombie. A sew seconds later his face drained of color as he stared over the tops of their heads. "Who's that dancing with Gwen?" he shouted.

Eloise and Sherry spun around in unison. Sherry shrieked and Eloise flew across the room. None of them had noticed his arrival. A minute later Derek was dancing in their group, right in front of Adam, who had a hard time believing it was the same person he had known in high school. All the intervening years he had pictured the scrawny boy, lying on the ground, his dyed blond hair in disarray, his broken glasses in the grass catching the glare from a nearby streetlight. The person in front of him channelled one of the hunky older models in a Cialis commercial about to take advantage of the right moment. His solid frame stretched the seams of his sport jacket and filled his tight jeans. His hair was thick, salt and pepper, and he wore a neatly trimmed beard. The neck of his button-down shirt was open, showing chest hair.

Adam's dancing faded to an anemic side step. His arms changed into lead pipes he could barely lift. Derek shimmied confidently until he was facing Adam. "Hello, Adam."

"Derek." Handshake? Fist pump? Definitely not a hug.

"Nice to see you."

"Likewise."

"Later." Derek returned to Sherry and whispered something in her ear.

Eloise had drifted to the front of the stage, and as she danced, kept glancing at the guitar player, who returned her looks with a smile. The song ended and the crowd showed appreciation with clapping and hooting. The female singer thanked them while the guitar player moved to the edge of the stage and leaned down to share a few words with Eloise. Sherry and Derek continued talking in low voices as the band launched into the next song, "On the Radio." Adam remembered disco dancing to the Donna Summer song in the 1980s.

"I bet you remember this one," said Derek, moving closer to Adam.

"New York, The Saint, around 1980, high on mushrooms. Oh yeah, I remember."

"I was in LA around that time. How far we've come!" Derek swept his arms taking in the surroundings.

Adam laughed and promptly noticed all the others in their group had disappeared. They were two men dancing together at the VFW in their hometown. "I don't think we can do this."

Derek suggested a drink and they headed to the bar.

The still waters of the lake reflected a half moon and the lights from the hospital and the large homes on Lake Shore Drive across the way. Crickets chirped outside the windows and the humidity coated everything so heavily a thunderstorm might have recently passed through. Adam and Derek sat in the front seat of Derek's rental car. By the time they left the VFW, it was clear Derek was in much better shape to drive. "I'll pick my car up in the morning," said Adam.

The lake was so much a part of their hometown, a reservoir supplying homes and industry, but it also fed and taunted the soul of the city. It gave life and had taken a few in accidents and drownings. Adam remembered boating and waterskiing there, joking about the pollution before people realized how serious it was. And everyone remembered icy nights in winter losing control of the wheels while crossing one of its bridges. Two of their classmates had plunged from the bridge into the frigid water.

In the silence of the car, the memories rippled through Adam's head foggy from too much booze and pot. He felt bewildered that he was sitting next to Derek in a parked car on the edge of the lake of his childhood.

Neither of them had wanted to go home after the VFW, prompting the detour to the lake, and yet they spoke little, perhaps overwhelmed by the thousands of things they might have said.

"This is weird," said Adam.

Derek pulled his eyes from the lake to look at Adam. "That's the best you got."

"I know I owe you a huge apology."

"I'm not here for that. It would have meant something years ago, but now..."

"It was so fucked up, I can't even begin—"

"Stop. I really don't want to go back there."

"Then why are we here."

Derek chuckled. "This is going to sound strange, but I wanted you to see me, to see I'm fine, great actually. I recently retired from thirty-five years working in the diplomatic corps, got to live all over the world, explore other cultures. I managed to dodge the HIV bullet. I'm healthy. I've had a number of loving relationships, none that lasted long-term, but I have no regrets. I own a home in Long Beach. Next year I'm publishing a memoir of my experiences overseas as a gay diplomat."

With each of Derek's revelations, Adam cowered under the feeling he had done relatively little with his life. And he got the message that as painful as the senseless beating was for Derek at the time, he had survived and possibly made stronger for it.

"I'm happy for you. I really am. You seem to be proof that living well is the best revenge."

"And you?"

"I'm married. Retired from being a community college counselor. My husband and I took our wrinkled asses to Palm Springs to join all the other wrinkled asses. The desert has its charms. My blood has grown so thin not sure I could live anywhere else."

"That sounds nice."

"Hah! He's having an affair with a younger guy. I don't know if we'll survive it."

"I'm over there from time to time. It would have been funny if I'd run into you."

"I swear you could have walked right by me and I wouldn't have recognized you. I *would* have noticed that you're a hot dude however."

Derek let out a bitter chuckle. "I appreciate the comment. It doesn't mean as much to me now as it used to."

"Oh, come on. A compliment never gets old."

A car of rowdy teenagers pulled into the space next to them, the stereo blaring Kanye West. Both Adam and Derek tensed up, a visceral reaction for gay men confronted with a gang of kids at night in an isolated area. One of them threw a beer bottle out the window. Adam turned to look at the youths.

"What are you looking at?" said the driver of the other car. The three other boys in the car laughed.

Adam turned back to Derek. "Don't you love it, surly white punks listening to Kanye West?"

"You say something?" the driver asked.

Derek started the car, but before he could back up, the teenagers had jumped out, rushed to Adam's door, and yanked it open. "I asked you a question," said the youth with blond curly hair and a scraggily beard.

"Fuck you!" said Adam.

The next moment the blond and another youth had pulled Adam out of the car. They had him on the ground and were on top of him. Blondie punched Adam in the face as he struggled to throw them off. The two other boys stood back and cheered them on.

Derek jumped out of the car. "Get off him!"

"Ooh, the boyfriend is mad," said one of the boys.

Derek landed a swift side kick to the shoulder of Blondie, sending him sprawling onto the gravel. The other kid, a short stocky boy, rushed Derek with a head butt. Derek knocked him aside and chopped him in the back. One of the other boys rushed to join the fight and Adam, still prone, grabbed his leg, causing him to tumble to the ground. Adam stood up, his head spinning, but he joined Derek as they faced the four boys. By this time Blondie was upright and rushed Derek, who used a karate kick to knock him back. The stocky youth had gotten behind Derek and jumped on his back, bringing him to his knees. Derek ducked his head, reached back, and flipped the youth onto the ground. Adam was not a fighter, but when he saw Blondie getting up, he kicked him as hard as he could, bringing to mind how his foot had connected with Derek so many years before.

"Let's get out of here," said the boy who had not participated in the fight. "It's just a couple of old fags." It diverted the attention of the other three long enough for Adam and Derek to jump in the car Derek had left running. He put it in reverse and hastily backed up. Gravel shot up from the tires as they got back on the road. Derek saw in the rear view mirror that the boys had gotten in their car and were coming after them.

Adam bled from his nose and a cut above the eye. "Are you okay?" said Derek. He pulled a handkerchief out of his pocket and handed it to Adam.

"I'll live," said Adam in a shaky voice.

"I'm taking you to St. Mary's." The lights of the hospital twinkled in the distance, but the other car was coming up fast behind them. "Hold on. It could get bumpy." He put his foot on the gas of his rented Camry, hugged the steering wheel, and fixed his eyes on the road. By the time they reached the bridge, the hoodlums had disappeared from the mirror.

Adam's heart still raced, and he began to shake, the impact of the fight catching up with him, the realization it could have been so much worse. "What the hell was that back there?"

"What?"

"The karate shit."

"You can probably guess when I signed up for classes. After that night, I never wanted to be defenseless again. At least I wanted to be able to put up a good fight."

"You've turned into a real macho man."

"Don't worry. I can still camp it up with the girls."

Adam removed the handkerchief he'd been holding against the wound above his eyebrow and stared at the blob of blood it had soaked up. "Thank you. I probably don't deserve you saving my ass."

"It's scary how good it feels when you're able to cause pain to someone who's being an asshole."

"Are you hurt?"

"I'll probably have some bruises. God, we're old men. I can't believe we still have to put up with that shit."

Derek dropped him off at the emergency entrance and went to park the car. Adam hobbled through the glass doors. It seems he had twisted his ankle at some point, and his knees were shaky. The adrenaline was wearing off and his whole body ached. The receptionist told him there would be a wait. He sat in the plastic upholstered chair and shed a few tears in gratitude for what Derek had done.

Derek came in a few minutes later with his cell phone to his ear and sat down next to Adam. He described the youths and the car to the police, even remembered the first few letters of the license plate. He was precise, showing a good memory in the midst of bedlam, a person of intelligence and compassion. His blue linen shirt was torn, the breast pocket flapping down like a dog's tongue, and the knees of his khaki pants were soiled, but not a single hair of his head appeared out of place.

A couple of hours later, after Adam received seven stitches above his eye and they gave a report of the attack to an uncomfortable patrol officer who could have been a bit more sympathetic, Derek pulled into the parking lot at Adam's building, setting off a flood of sensor lights. They walked to the front of the building with Adam's arm on Derek's shoulders for support. Adam was in a great deal of pain, the numbing effects of the alcohol and marijuana having left his body and the pain medicine still not kicking in. Another sensor light helped them open the door.

"Pull the door tight," said Adam. "It scrapes."

More sensor lights banished the shadows from the long hallway, but not the dead silence, making Adam thankful he was not alone.

"Thanks for bringing me home," said Adam once they were inside the apartment. "I'm going to fix a drink. Would you like one?"

"Are you supposed to drink on those pain meds?"

Adam was touched by Derek's concern. "You don't have to take care of me anymore. I'm okay."

"A drink sounds good."

"Could you fix them? I'm going to change out of these bloody clothes. There's vodka and cranberry on the kitchen counter. I'll just have vodka on the rocks."

"Sounds good."

They sat on the sofa and sipped their drinks. It had started to rain and the drops pattered on the window behind them. Adam struggled to keep his eyes open. Within minutes, his head fell forward, and promptly jerked up as he caught himself.

"You should go to bed. I'll call you in the morning."

"You're welcome to the sofa," Adam said in a groggy voice. "Getting pretty nasty out there." A tree branch scraped against the window and the rain now pelted the glass.

"Thanks, I'll...yeah, good idea. I can take you to get your car in the morning."

Derek helped Adam into the bedroom. Adam kicked off his shoes, lay back on the mattress, and was asleep in two minutes. Derek found an extra pillow in the closet and stretched out on the sofa.

Lightning flashed across the sky, followed by rolling thunder. Adam's eyes sprang open. A man stood in the dark room, silhouetted against the window. Adam rose up and let out a nightmare bellow of a man condemned to death.

"It's only me, Adam. I came in to check on you. You were muttering in your sleep."

"I'm sorry. How stupid of me!"

"Don't worry about it. Are you okay?"

Adam lay back, and everything hit him at once, the attack of the surly boys, the undeserved kindness of Derek, the uncertainty of being in a place so full of unsettling memories far from what he now called home, and the pain of his husband leaving him. Tears rolled down his cheeks. In another moment he was choking on his sobs. Derek lay down on the bed. He pulled Adam to his chest and let him weep.

# Backlit

Sleep was sweet for Dwayne. When he could get it. Every night, as soon as he turned off the bedside lamp, his mind cranked up, buzz in the brain. It had been that way since the war, the one nobody talked about anymore, Vietnam. Nightmares of village atrocities, flares of a surprise attack, the smell; oh, the bouquet of napalm, frangipani, and death.

June was his savior. She waited for him, got an education while he went off to war. She didn't make the horror of his nights disappear, but having her by his side, someone who wasn't afraid of his darkness, smoothed the sharp edges. As he sat across from her in the low light of the restaurant in North Beach, just back from the war, feeling damaged and unlovable, he couldn't believe she still wanted to marry him like they had planned in high school.

June was goodness, soft and smart, full-figured with a funny little nose like a button mushroom. She would strike a pose in front of the mirror and laugh. "I'm not fat. I'm Rubenesque." After they made love, he would lie on top of her, his muscles untethering, sinking into her softness, becoming one with her. "Honey, I can't breathe," she would say. Rolling from his dream onto the cool mattress, he mumbled, "Sorry, babe."

He was going to group again, years after Vietnam, years after June was gone. A counselor had recently instructed the group in visualization. That moment of melting into June was his special place. Sometimes it worked. The ghouls in the shadows of the bedroom began to fade. His head sunk into the pillow. His body jerked once to catch himself from falling, and a short time later let go, his mind empty.

A motorcycle roared down the street and ripped the perfect fabric of his nothingness. His eyes snapped open. Movement on the other side of the bed filled him with an instant of bliss until the image of June was swiftly shattered by Beth's ebb-and-flow nasal breathing, more irritating than a snore.

June had saved him, given him a beautiful son, and nourished the child through his early years before a cruel God ripped her from his arms. The medication took her hair in clumps and the disease her voluptuous curves. He had survived the war and the return to an unforgiving country though he hadn't been sure if he could survive June's passing. But he did.

His brain was clicking again. He stared at the ceiling. A chill passed through the room. The motorcycle had sounded louder than it should have, like it could have ripped through the house from front to back. An urge rose up in Dwayne to strangle someone, the motorcycle rider, the clerk who had looked at him funny in the supermarket that afternoon, the telemarketer who called right before dinner. Why was a light on down the hall? Had Beth gotten up in the short time he had been asleep and forgotten to turn the bathroom light off?

A shadow filled the doorframe. Dwayne bristled with the precise panic he experienced so many times during the war at something emerging from the darkness. A baseball bat leaned between the bed and the wall. He reached for it and at the same moment heard the voice of his son. "Dad, I fucked up."

The words hung in the air like a foul smell, making it hard to breathe. Billy took a couple steps inside the room. Backlit by the light from the hall, his shoulders high and his hands stuffed in the pockets of his jacket, he appeared the big and strong son of a few years before when he was going to the gym. But the panic in his voice was a boy's, a distress call in the wilderness from someone who shared his blood. It took Dwayne back fifteen years to when his son was a frequent visitor to his room in the middle of the night. After his mom died, he would stand at the foot of the bed, a barefoot and skinny ten-year old, his eyes searching for comfort in the dark.

Dwayne sat up, the pull of hopelessness in his gut. He guessed Billy was high. Probably needed money. Since Billy dropped out of a drug rehab program a couple of months back, Dwayne had dealt with several of these late-night visits. But his immediate concern was to get him out of the room before Beth woke up.

Too late. She stirred and then shot up. "What the—?"

"It's all right, Beth. It's just Billy."

"Just Billy! I want him out of my bedroom and out of my house."

"I'll take care of it," he said. "Go back to sleep." He reached over and stroked her hair.

She moved away from his caress and pulled the covers up over her 49er T-shirt. "Now, Dwayne!"

Billy stood frozen in Beth's ire.

Dwayne threw back the comforter, swung his legs out, and jammed his feet in his slippers. He hurried over to Billy and took his arm. "What's going on, Billy?" His arm felt bony inside the puffy jacket and Dwayne realized the bulkiness he had perceived earlier was only the down jacket he had taken to wearing in recent months. A down jacket in August wasn't right, even in San Francisco's cool summers.

He turned his son toward the door, but Billy glanced back over his shoulder at Beth, his mouth hanging open. He stared at her, though his eyes floated, carrying no weight.

"Jesus!" she said in a breathy hiss. When they had cleared the threshold, Beth got out of bed and slammed the door. The lock clicked and Billy's body jumped. He began to moan, a barely audible kind of rumble from deep inside.

In the light of the hall, Billy's face was shiny with sweat. "Come on, let's go in the kitchen," said Dwayne.

He moved his son as if he were an invalid, his sneakers scratching on the worn brown carpet, past the bathroom light toward the front of the house. The front door stood wide open, and air off the ocean rode in on the yellowish light from the street, tickling Dwayne's bare ankles. He propped Billy against the wall while he went to close it, leaning his shoulder against the heavy door, and then pausing at the sight of a strange car in the driveway, a red Corolla. He stuck his head out and gazed up and down the street before easing the wood into its frame.

In the kitchen Dwayne flipped on the light.

Billy's hands shot up to his eyes as if they had been doused with acid. "No, Dad. No. Cut it."

He put out the light, but the kitchen remained illuminated by a cool silver glow from an almost full moon shining in the window over the sink. "Can I get you something to eat?"

"Just some water," he said in a scratchy whisper.

"Whose car is that?"

"I borrowed it." He wobbled on his feet, and promptly fell into a chair at the table.

"From who?"

"Some lady."

"What's that supposed to mean? Some lady?"

He shrugged, and in a deliberate move, pulled a snub nose revolver out of an inside pocket and placed it on the table so carefully it made silent contact with the Formica. "I didn't hurt her, but I had to get away. The police were coming."

Dwayne stared at the gun, but tried to remain calm. "The police?"

"I tried to rob a bank."

In the dim light he searched Billy's eyes, but he didn't waste time trying to decide if he was lying. He set the glass of water on the table near the gun. "Billy, we got two things on the agenda. First, give me the gun. And then we've got to get that car out of here."

Billy grabbed the pistol and returned it to the dark place inside his jacket. The water jiggled in the glass with his sudden movement. He patted the hard place where the metal lay against his chest and smacked his lips a couple of times before a low, dreamy voice emerged from his lips. "She had those dangly earrings like Mom used to wear." He wiped the back of his hand across his mouth and then used his thumb and forefinger to smooth out the corner of his grimace, a gesture bringing June back from the grave. He had her eyes, too. Pain cut through Dwayne as he remembered her quiet, intense look that used to leave him uneasy, and yet comforted him with its familiarity.

"The lady said, 'I know you're a good boy. Don't do this.'" He made a high imitation of her voice, and let out a twisted little laugh. "She didn't even act scared."

"Should she have been?" Dwayne wanted to humor Billy and keep him talking. He wasn't a bad kid. His life had gotten off track.

Billy's eyes bugged out and he scratched the back of his head, followed by the eerie laugh again. He scratched and laughed. When the laugh stopped, in the dead quiet of the kitchen still smelling of fried chicken, the scratch was audible, like a dog's paw moving across its hindquarters.

"Okay, then, give me the keys to the car," Dwayne said as if proposing a game. He sat down at the table and crossed his hands in front of him.

Billy stared at something behind his father and didn't answer. His eyes were so full of pupil there was hardly any blue in them.

Dwayne waved his hands in front of Billy's face, trying to get him to focus. "Hey, the keys. Where are they?"

Billy scratched, and then his body twitched like someone had dropped an ice cube down his back. Outside the window, the lights of a car went by and he jerked his head toward the fleeting glare. Then the low creepy moan was back.

"Are they in the car? We've got to move it. We'll take it over and leave it by the park."

For a second, he was back from his drugged wasteland with a grin showing hints of the old Billy. He spoke in a smoother voice. "Guess you know something about abandoning cars."

In the pit his life became after June's death, Dwayne couldn't be bothered by moving his car for street cleaning or putting money in meters. Tickets accumulated on his windshield. It got so bad they put a boot on his wheels. It was cheaper to walk away and buy an old clunker. He went through a number of cars in that manner, all abandoned throughout the city.

Billy's silly grin made Dwayne's face soften, a father's gaze. He remembered what a funny kid he had been, a prankster always up to something, driving his mother nuts. As a boy he would hide things like the newspaper or the remote control and make them guess where it was. Nothing mean. He would do sweet things, too, like bring his mother flowers. Yet there was always the glint in his eye he was banking his good acts to counter the upcoming bad ones.

"Yeah, well, we need the keys," Dwayne said. Billy's grin instantly faded behind the pale desperation that had taken over his life the past couple of years. The drugs, cocaine and crack mostly, were close to putting out the last spark of humor in his eyes. He went back to scratching and twitching, swiped his hand across his mouth removing imaginary spit.

"Maybe you left them in the car. Let's go check."

"I need some money, Dad," he said in barely audible voice.

"I'm not buying you drugs."

"Just until next week. Some clients are gonna pay me."

"You still have clients?"

"Yeah. Lots."

Dwayne knew it was a lie. Billy's landscaping business had suffered in the last year—unfinished jobs, unanswered calls, angry clients. Dwayne had tried to help him with some of the work until Beth had a fit. She reminded him he had his own life to take care of, and the only thing he was doing was supporting Billy's habit.

"I thought you and Jason were getting clean."

At the mention of Jason, he bolted from the chair and went to the sink. He wrapped his hands around the frame of the sink for support. "You don't get it," he said.

"Get what? Are you getting clean or not?"

"You don't just snap your fingers. Man, it's got to be slow. Step at a time. I gotta...please. I'll pay you back. I swear."

Dwayne stared at a worn spot on the Formica tabletop. "Things are tough right now. Can't you ask Jason? You said he was rich."

Again Billy looked struck and put his hands over his face, moving them down across his cheeks, stretching the dehydrated skin over the bones of his skull. He dropped his hands and sighed. "He's broke. His ex is bleeding him dry."

Jason was a client of Billy's who he met when he was called to do a landscaping job around a small cottage near the Castro. Every time Dwayne saw Billy after that, it was Jason this and Jason that. Billy was doing coke at the time and Dwayne hoped the guy, being a psychiatrist, might be a good influence. His hopes had soon been dashed. Since Billy and Jason got together, his son had gotten worse, more jumpy and wild-eyed. He guessed they were both doing drugs, feeding on each other's habits.

Dwayne and Billy went out to the Corolla. Inside the car Dwayne got a better look at Billy's face in the overhead light. It had a yellow tinge and there was a bruise under his left eye. Jason had probably hit him again.

"That's quite a shiner you got."

"It's nothing." He pointed to the keys in the ignition. "There they are. Let's go."

Dwayne backed the car out of the driveway and peered up at the window to see Beth draw back the curtain, a sentinel guarding over her castle. It was her house, but he hated it when she threw it in his face. He'd had his own house once, in his other life, before Beth. When Billy's mother got sick, the first thing they lost was her insurance. Then it was the savings, the house, and his auto body shop in that order. If the treatments had worked, he wouldn't have minded losing everything. But she was gone in about six months.

Dwayne was forced to go work for somebody else, in a repair shop for Japanese cars out in the Excelsior. By the time Billy was fifteen, Dwayne had saved enough to move them from a studio in the Tenderloin to a decent two-bedroom off Silver Avenue. Dwayne met Beth a couple years later at a singles party. People were playing mingling games. Dwayne and Beth stood in a corner, drawn to each other by their jaws hanging equally aghast at the party antics. A couple of Dwayne's off-color remarks made her laugh.

Dwayne and Billy moved in with Beth, and Dwayne rationalized he was doing it at least in part for Billy, that he was giving him something close to a normal family. But it was a disaster from the beginning. Billy refused to eat the first dinner Beth prepared. He excused himself and went to his new room, which he had already announced he hated. He had changed from a normal, rambunctious kid before his mother's death to a moody and reclusive teenager that Dwayne hardly knew. But the teenage Billy was nothing compared to the fractured young man sitting next to him in the car. It was the second time in his life he had been left in a pool of helplessness, watching a loved one descend into a consuming hell. But he still had hope for Billy. He was alive. Things could turn around.

"Let's go," his son said, bouncing his fist on his knee. "We can stop at the ATM over on Geary."

Dwayne had a sinking feeling Billy wasn't going to give up on the money. "Put your seatbelt on. We don't want to get stopped in this piece of crap car. Christ! A Corolla. With my luck it probably has a taillight out or something."

Dwayne drove slowly down the quiet street, periodically glancing at Billy. "You were shitting me about robbing a bank, right?"

"God's truth. I told ya I need money," he said in a

jittery staccato. "Gave the teller a note. Said I had a gun. He stared at me and laughed."

"You're too damn good-looking. That's your problem," Dwayne said with a splintery chuckle. Billy was boyishly handsome. Even with the goatee he looked a lot younger than his 25 years. The girls had been crazy about him in high school. He was smart, too. If he got himself cleaned up, there would be nothing and nobody he couldn't have. Why he had chosen Jason was a mystery to Dwayne.

Dwayne had met Billy and Jason for dinner a few months back, and after the dinner he told Beth, "It didn't take me two minutes to determine he was full of shit, even with his fancy car and diplomas up the ass. He told me some bull crappy nonsense about reading in a ding-a-ling Chinese book his real soulmate wasn't his wife, but someone like Billy. Not Billy. Someone like him. Christ! I wanted to punch the guy in the face."

"You've got to accept Billy's gay and get over it," said Beth. It was her usual unsentimental practicality.

"Hell, I got over that a long time ago." He didn't say it, but he had accepted Billy was gay because it was what June would have wanted. Billy was all he had left of her and he didn't want to lose him. In high school Billy had taken up with a friend, the only friend he had, a rake thin kid who wore a lot of black, let his hair grow, and smoked pot. Dwayne let it go on—the pot smoking, the hanging out in Billy's room for hours, the friend spending the night. It made Billy appear happier, less lost.

Billy had a few good years. In his senior year of high school, he surprised his dad by inviting a girl down the street to go to the prom. He went to college, graduated, and got his landscaping business going with a well-designed website. His business was successful and he started dating a girl he had met at UC Davis, at least that's what he had told Dwayne. A short time later his anxiety had returned.

When Dwayne realized Billy was having problems with his business, he got him to agree to a monthly dinner at a dive steakhouse they liked in the Outer Mission called Geneva Steak. The place had been around forever, and despite the tacky décor, the food was good. One of the last times they got together was shortly after he had met Jason. At the door of the restaurant, Billy announced he and Jason were going to Hawaii the following weekend.

Dwayne twisted his mouth and it clicked as he spoke. "Whoa, buddy, now you're going on vacation with a client, a man recently divorced from his wife?"

"That's why he needs to get away and I do too."

At the table Billy's eyes darted all over the place and he got up twice to go to the bathroom before they got their salads. The second time he came back to the table, he fixed his gaze on the salad like it was a bowl of worms. He waved the fork above the greens at the speed his mind was going, but without eating a single leaf.

He returned to babbling, Jason this and Jason that. "Jason has this theory about cleansing your soul. You have to go down to the lower reaches of hell and come face to face with your devils before you can come back into the light."

"Uh-huh," Dwayne said.

Between the salad and the steaks, Billy went out for a cigarette. Dwayne ordered another scotch and watched the family at the next table with three kids under the age of six. The mother was a frazzled thirty-something with a short fuse. As soon as she got one quieted down, another would go into crisis. The father sat like a baboon at the zoo, in a daze, giving useless quips when she appealed to him for help. Dwayne had to force himself not to get up and shake the guy, tell him to wake up to what he had.

Billy came back in and slumped in the chair. He reeked of tobacco. "Instead of cleansing your soul, you better think about cleansing your bloodstream," Dwayne said.

"What's that supposed to mean?"

"You know damn well what I mean. You're high as a fucking kite."

The waiter set a bloody T-bone in front of Billy and he shuddered like he'd just witnessed a murder. "I think I'm going to become a vegetarian like Jason."

"Sure. That oughta solve everything."

"You're so negative. Every time I talk about Jason you sneer. You only met him that one time. You hate him."

"I hate what he's doing to you. Look at yourself."

"I'll wait in the car." He stood up and walked to the door with his hands buried in the pockets of his down jacket, which he hadn't bothered to take off the whole time they were in the restaurant.

"Billy, come on."

Dwayne paid the bill and went out to the car.

Since that night at the restaurant, things had gotten worse, apparently to the point he attempted to rob a bank and stole a car. As many times as Dwayne told himself that he couldn't keep supporting Billy's habit, he couldn't stand to see the agony his son was going through. He stopped at the cash machine and gave him a hundred. They ditched the car over by Golden Gate Park and Billy took off into the fog with the money. He promised to call his dad in a couple of days.

Three days passed without Dwayne hearing from him. He left several messages and got no response. On a foggy morning he sat at the kitchen table leafing through the paper. He picked up a coffee cup and held it for its warmth. Beth had already gone to her job at Safeway. Through the steam rising above the cup he caught a page three headline: "Psychiatrist Meets Gruesome End." A squiggly pain overtook him. He wasn't sure if he was having a heart attack or only an acidic gurgle from the coffee. He scanned the article in an instant, going right to Jason's name. They described a bloody crime scene and the squalor of the cottage. A neighbor had smelled a foul odor and heard a dog whining. The police said the body had probably been there about three days, the same three days it had been since Billy had shown up at his home. Dwayne bounced out of the chair and went to the sink on the verge of puking.

His hand shook when he picked up the phone to call his boss. He told him he had an emergency and wouldn't be in until later. He jumped in his car and raced over to Billy's apartment. The article had said the authorities had leads but hadn't arrested anyone. He hoped to get there before the police.

Billy didn't answer the door, but Dwayne knew where he hid a key and let himself in. The first time he had seen Billy's decorated apartment, he kidded him it was a bit fancy-shmancy for his taste. He needed to man it up with a little dirt. Now the chic décor was buried under old pizza boxes with cold, half-eaten slices, coke cans with cigarette ashes around the rim, and piles of dirty clothes.

He was sprawled out on his bed with his clothes on and Dwayne's knees buckled under the notion he was dead. But he checked his son's breathing as he learned to do in Vietnam, and he was alive. He sat on the bed and lifted Billy's dull weight toward him. He held him a minute before he began landing little slaps on either side of his face. "Billy, wake up!"

Billy groaned and tried to open his eyes but couldn't. Dwayne dragged him into the shower and turned on the cold water.

"Shit!" Billy said. He shook his head like a wet dog and flailed his arms, landing a good punch on the side of his father's head. It took him a couple of minutes to realize where he was and what was happening. When he came to, he had a lucid moment, and promptly slumped onto the floor. "Leave me alone. It's all over."

"I know what happened. It was self-defense. He beat you."

"No. I killed him. Couldn't stand it anymore. He said he was going back to his wife."

Dwayne grabbed and shook him. "It was an accident, damn it! You're not a killer. My boy is not a killer. They'll understand. You've got to turn yourself in."

"I did it," he mumbled, trying to push his dad away. "Can't you see? I wanted him dead. It was the only way to end it."

Dwayne stood up. "Come on. We're going someplace."

"Where?" Billy said with the tiniest spark of interest in his voice.

When Dwayne was going through a hard time a few years back, Beth convinced him to see someone at her church. He had never been a churchgoing man, but the minister had gotten under his skin, in a good way. He had the gift of talking to people, and Dwayne would try anything to help Billy.

He took Billy by the arm and lifted him to his feet. "I want you to talk to someone. We can't wait around here until the police come."

Billy gazed at his dad through puffy half-open eyes. It appeared Dwayne had gotten through to him and his mind was beginning to work. "Okay," he said. "Let me change. My clothes are all wet."

He made a move toward his closet and Dwayne grabbed his arm. "You need to give me the gun. This time I mean it."

Again he stared at his father as if he wasn't quite sure what he was talking about. "Don't worry. I got rid of it."

"Good."

A few minutes later he shuffled into the living room wearing his down jacket and an SF baseball cap. They went out to Dwayne's faded green Volvo and drove over to First Congregational on Polk. He parked in front and made sure he stuffed the meter with all the coins he could find, even fished out a quarter stuck between the seat and the console. The minister wasn't in, so they went back to the car and waited. Dwayne got some coffee from a place across the street.

"It's going to be all right," Dwayne said. "We'll get a good lawyer."

Billy sipped his coffee and stared out the window.

"He didn't treat you right. He abused you. You've still got the bruise. They'll believe you." Dwayne pushed the buttons to put both their windows down halfway. Billy had a smell like sour milk. The dousing he had given him earlier was likely the first time he had seen the shower in a week.

Billy broke his silence. "Why did he say he was going to buy cigarettes? I fell asleep on the couch waiting for him to come back. He was gone the whole night. Probably with his ex. She couldn't handle him being with me, refused to meet me. Fine if that was what he wanted, but why lie about it? Came back in the morning and tried to act like nothing happened, some shitty half grin on his face. His hair was still wet from a shower. Just went in his room and got fucked up. I wanted to forget about it, but I couldn't. It kept growing in my head until I thought I would explode. His shitty grin was killing me, like he was playing with me." His voice had the same painful quality of sludge being forced through a rusty pipe. It was like his dying mother trying to talk through her ravaged throat, and it broke Dwayne's heart.

"You don't have to go on, Billy. It's okay."

"It's not okay. Let me talk. Sorry, Dad. This is so fucked up." He paused and took a sip of coffee. "I picked up a coffee table book, lots of pale flowers on it, French Impressionists or something, and went into the bedroom.

He was sitting on the bed with the crack pipe in his mouth. Didn't even look up. I banged him on the back of the head so hard he fell onto the floor. I dropped the book, and then kicked him in the stomach."

"You didn't know what you were doing,"

"Oh, I knew. Been thinking about it all night. He looked up from the floor like he didn't recognize me. I kicked him again, don't know how many times. His face pinched up and relaxed, pinched up and relaxed. He didn't care. Seemed like he wanted me to hurt him. He was going to have the last laugh. And he burst into laughter. Laughed like a crazy man. I couldn't stand it. Blood trickled out of the corner of his mouth. I yelled at him to get up and fight. He kept laughing. If he had done the tiniest thing to try to stop me, I think I would have stopped. All he did was laugh and cough up blood, so I picked up the lamp from the bedside table and bashed his head. From there I don't know. I gawked at myself from above, in a nightmare, watched myself hit him with the ceramic base of the lamp until it shattered. Blood was flying. I felt warm drops on my face. I tasted it on my lips."

Dwayne had seen death, war death, intestines spilled out and body parts on the jungle grass. But hearing his son tell the story, the crazed avoidable violence of it, made him sicker than anything he had ever seen or heard. His gut was locked in a tight knot and his jaw ached.

He stared out the windshield in a daze, only half-noticing a panhandler weaving toward the car. Billy gaped at his father with a mangled contentment at his confession.

"Hey," the panhandler said at Billy's window, and then mumbled something through bruised teeth. Billy stabbed the button and put the glass up in his face without looking at him. The man proceeded to rant, accusing them of being agents of the devil, his voice becoming distant as the window locked into its groove. He looked like a guy Dwayne had known in Vietnam, and he felt sorry for him.

"Let's get out of here," Billy growled.

"There's no danger. Ignore him." Dwayne still imagined in a few minutes they would go into the church and find the minister who would help Billy see the logic of turning himself in.

"Go!" he screamed.

"Okay. Take it easy." The moment Dwayne turned the key, he saw a patrol car across the street slow to a crawl. The officer on the driver's side reworked his fresh young face into a serious stare in the direction of the lunatic shouting and gesticulating outside their window. Dwayne looked at the cop and put on a weak smile, throwing up his arms in question. Beside him Billy moved, and he bumped his father with his elbow as he clambered over the seat into the back. "What are you doing?" Dwayne yelled, but swiftly turned back to the cop with the pathetic smile still on his face. The police car had stopped, and the two officers got out. In the rear view mirror Dwayne saw his son stretched out face down on the back seat with the jacket over his head.

The second officer was a tall, solidly built Black woman with her hair straightened and pulled back so tight in a ponytail it took all expression out of her face. They walked over, and the young blond man motioned for Dwayne to put the window the rest of the way down. The panhandler had abandoned his tirade and shuffled up the street. The cops seemed uninterested in him. The male officer told him to turn off the engine and step outside the car with his driver's license and registration.

Dwayne fought to keep his voice steady, but in the pit of his stomach was a burning sense of hopelessness. "There's no problem. It was only a panhandler."

The cop repeated his request and the woman walked around to the other side of the car. She leaned down and stared into the back seat.

Dwayne got out and gave him the documents.

"Who's in the back seat?"

"It's my son. He had a rough night. He's really beat."

The officer studied the license before making a sign to the woman. They met at the front of the car and talked in low voices while Dwayne leaned against the car and gazed blankly at the gawking people in cars going by. With the license in hand, the woman ran over to the patrol car and got on the radio. She set his license on the dashboard, picked up a Starbucks coffee cup, and in a routine movement, took a drink. Then she proceeded to talk into the radio.

The cop with the boyish face came back and stood next to Dwayne. He looked like he had just come from a haircut, every hair in place. "We should get out of the street," he said, and took Dwayne's arm. "Come over to the other side of the car." As they moved toward the sidewalk he glanced into the car several times and appeared satisfied Billy had not moved. He put Dwayne against the car and did the spread and search.

"I was in Vietnam," Dwayne said without knowing why. "I served my country."

The woman officer came back across the street. The traffic stopped to let her pass. Her blank face had not changed, but the tone of her voice was full of new information. "Is your son William Ehrens of 2304 Harrison St.?" she said. Out the corner of his eye, Dwayne saw her make a sign to her partner to keep him against the car.

"Yes, but—"

"Is he armed?"

"No. He's in trouble. I admit it. He's a good kid. There's an explanation."

"We have to get him out of the car." With a look and another sign, she communicated the seriousness of the situation to her partner.

"I'll do the honors," said the man.

The woman took a grip on Dwayne's arm and led him away from the car. A crowd had formed and she told them to move back. The young cop drew his gun and yanked open the back door. Dwayne stared at the soles of Billy's sneakers hanging over the edge of the seat. He remembered how as a kid he used to fall asleep with his sneakers on. He would go in and take them off but let him sleep in his clothes. Billy hated being woken up.

"Hey," the cop said, shaking Billy's leg. "You need to get out of the car." Authority vibrated in his voice.

"Billy, get up!" Dwayne said and tried to move forward. The woman pulled him back with a jerk.

"Get out of the car," said the male cop. He grabbed Billy's legs and pulled them. Billy started to kick just before there was a flash and a loud pop in the dim light of the back seat. At first Dwayne believed the cop had shot

Billy, but the officer fell back and landed on the pavement.

"No!" Dwayne screamed and lunged forward, breaking the woman's grip. But she expertly hit him from behind and knocked him to the pavement. She got on top of him with a knee in his back. "Brad, are you all right?" she shouted to her partner.

"Yeah." And nodding at Dwayne, "Break his balls. He fucking lied about the gun."

Then it struck Dwayne like a bat in his head it had been Billy's gun that had gone off. Billy had shot himself.

The woman cuffed Dwayne in a single gesture.

"I didn't know," Dwayne grunted. "He told me he got rid of it."

The young cop was on his feet with his gun pointed at Billy. "Drop the gun and get out! Hands on your head!"

Billy rolled over and put his feet on the ground. He stood up and was on the curb, hands in the air. For a moment Dwayne imagined everything was okay. Billy had that silly smile on his face. A moment later he recoiled in horror at the sight of blood on the side of his head, the hole where the bullet had entered his skull. Billy took a step toward his dad and fell. A woman from the crowd screamed. Sirens from different directions converged on them in a deafening shriek.

Dwayne and Billy both lay on the sidewalk with their faces against the concrete, five feet away from each other, looking into each other's eyes.

Billy's pupils were losing light, and his eyelids fluttered the way his mother's had when she was leaving him. "Don't go, Billy," Dwayne whispered. His heart was shredded into tiny pieces. He had failed again to save someone he loved.

The male cop announced he had the gun from the back seat, and Dwayne sensed a lightening of the pressure on his back. He got up on his knees and crawled over to Billy. He was still cuffed, so he laid his head on his son's back. Billy's heart was pumping.

In seconds the horror changed to the crispness of a medical scene with people in uniforms swarming over Billy, flashing lights, orders between people with blue plastic gloves, IV's, a stretcher. The woman officer raised Dwayne up on his feet. She undid his cuffs and put him in the back of the ambulance. He held Billy's cold hand, and the chill went straight to his heart.

Beth touched Dwayne's shoulder and his eyes sprang open. The impossible had happened. He had fallen asleep in the hospital waiting room while Billy was in surgery.

"You okay?" she said.

He shook his head. "I want to change things, Beth. I want to have an effect. Everything comes out...wrong."

Beth dropped her shoulders. He took her hand and held it to his cheek.

"I don't know," continued Dwayne. "If he makes it, I'm gonna do my damnedest..."

"Either way is not going to be easy."

"Don't be mad at me. I couldn't give up on him. He's my son."

She fell into the couch beside him. "I know." Her voice was full of her own regrets.

They looked up and saw a doctor coming toward them.

# Blade of Grass

Camera in hand, lanyard dangling from my neck, I enter the stadium through the special entrance for the press. Someone shouts and motions for me to get down so I'm not blocking the view. I fall to my knees on the green grass and am immediately mesmerized by a close-up view of thirty to forty Turkish men, naked to the waist, olive-skinned and muscular, marching barefoot across the field, torsos glistening with oil. Their bouncy steps are in sync with the thundering beat of drums and the piercing wail of a wind instrument called a *zurna*. I snap pictures in rapid succession.

A few steps out onto the field, the wrestlers take a knee, reach down with one hand to touch the ground, and then in a quick motion touch their chest, lips and forehead. They continue strutting around the arena, find their designated partner, and begin the matches. I crawl in the grass as close as I can to the nearest pair. A referee waves me back to a distance other photographers are respecting, and I wriggle my body backward while stopping every few feet to snap photos.

To arrive at this magical place, I only had to show my editor five minutes of a YouTube video about the annual

Kirkpinar Wrestling Championships in Edirne, Turkey. The editor offered me little in terms of expenses, but he enthusiastically embraced my project to photograph and write an article for the magazine. I imagined my friends from high school seeing my byline and being amused at me covering a wrestling event. In school, I felt pressured to choose a sport, and convinced myself wrestling would be a cool option. I suppose, deep down, it was simply a desire for male contact. Big mistake. I was horrible at it. My weight group always pitted tall, skinny me with someone short and compact. Gangly against nimble, I lost every time. My teenage nickname, Beetie, didn't come from my red hair as many believed, but the way my face turned crimson from the effort of wrestling and the red splotches on my skin where I had been held and squeezed. Years later and with an adult's heightened appreciation of the male body, I stumbled across a video about Turkish Oil Wrestling. The mark the wrestling nightmare had left on my brain was promptly erased, and I was soon on my way to the other side of the world to cover the event.

I am now prone on the field, shooting through the high grass. I try to block out the other journalists and the bleachers filled with fans, imagining I am in the wild, as I was the summer before, on safari in Africa. I think of the wildebeests I photographed, butting heads as the two wrestlers touch foreheads and put their arms on each other's shoulders. They walk around in circles. One reaches out and grabs the waistband of his opponent. Since their bodies have been slathered with oil before the match begins, each participant is looking for a way to get a grip on his partner in order to flip him and pin him on his back. Another match on the field has already come to this conclusion after only a few minutes.

All the wrestlers wear leather breeches tied at the waist, hanging low on their hips, and reaching down to their knees. In the back just below the waist, the leather is tooled and decorated with metal studs spelling out their names. In the match I'm watching, it is Ibrahim versus Tarkan. Ibrahim has a mustache on a rugged but kind face; I'm betting on him.

Ibrahim gets a grip on Tarkan's waist and an intense struggle ensues, landing them both on the ground. Ibrahim is on top, but Tarkan manages to slip from under him and get behind him. Tarkan leans down on Ibrahim's back, crotch to butt, arm reaching under his chest to grab Ibrahim's left arm. Tarkan changes tactics and slides his arm deep inside the waistband of Ibrahim's pants, wedging it along his thigh. I gasp. My camera goes *snap, snap, snap*. Is this legal? The other pairs on the field are doing the same thing.

Muscles strain, positions change, grunts and grimaces. The sun beats down without mercy. After twenty minutes of constant flip-flopping, the two fighters suddenly stop as if by mutual agreement. They kneel and fall back on their heels. They stare into the distance, catching their breaths and wiping sweat from their brows. Blades of grass are stuck to their backs. And then Ibrahim's gaze falls directly on me, possibly drawn by the constant click of my camera. He tilts his head in question. A smile flashes.

The line of sight is then interrupted by a referee running over with a group of water and oil boys. It is a break. Each of the fighters stands up, takes a can of water, and pours it over his head, letting the water cascade over oily shoulders, down over glistening pectoral muscles, running over hairy navels before disappearing into the darkness of their breeches.

It is time to oil up again. For a moment, they are no longer adversaries, but comrades oiling each other's backs. I feel a pang of jealousy. The fight continues. My guy looks refreshed, while Tarkan's energy is gone. Now it is Ibrahim who wedges his arm into the pants of the other, and with one swift motion, lifts him up and drops him on the ground, falling on top of him. The match is over; my guy has won. The referee holds up the winner's hand. The two fighters hug. Over Tarkan's shoulder, Ibrahim's eyes seem to lock onto mine again. His smile is now victorious. I still can't believe he is looking at me and I turn around to see if there is a wife or girlfriend in the stands. When I look back toward the field, they have left and joined a large group of wrestlers who have finished their matches or are waiting for their chance to enter the field. Many are sprawled on the ground, leaning against a chain link fence, their arms draped over the shoulders of their fellows. Others are sitting in front of their friends, wedged between their legs, leaning strong backs against sweaty chests. When people see the pictures they are going to ask if they are all gay, and I will have to explain what I have learned in my travels throughout the Middle East (sometimes the hard way) that male affection, as endearing as it is, has little to do with being gay. I look for my guy. I have a fantasy of talking to him, turning the conversation to ask if he would model for me, knowing full well the words would only stick in my throat.

He has disappeared. I go back to taking pictures and spend the rest of the afternoon getting grass stains on my khakis. I see many examples of Olympic male beauty, but none of them interest me in the way Ibrahim did. In the evening I walk the streets, gazing in the windows of every restaurant and café, strolling through hotel lobbies, looking for the smile that so captured me. Though I recognize many of the wrestlers, Ibrahim is nowhere to be found. I finish the night drinking too many beers in the hotel bar and get up late. I miss the morning matches. When I see Ibrahim walking with a towel around his shoulders toward the exit on the other side of the stadium, I realize I have missed his match and I bang my thigh with my fist.

The final day is filled with ceremony and medals and cheers and smiles. But I am hung over again, and miserable because Ibrahim has disappeared. If I could simply talk to him a minute, maybe have tea with him at one of the small cafes, I would be completely happy. The event comes to a close and the exodus of wrestlers begins, back to their hometowns across the country, back to their mothers and wives and girlfriends. In hopes of running into Ibrahim, I have booked the hotel for one extra night and spend the morning hanging around the bus station, watching the wrestlers get on various buses back to their hometowns, until people begin to look at me suspiciously. Accepting my defeat, I rent a scooter with the intention of seeing some ruins outside the city, an Ottoman palace built when Edirne was the capital of the empire in the fourteenth and fifteenth centuries.

Going down a hill with a curve at the bottom, still thinking about Ibrahim and missed opportunities, I lose control and go off into the gravel. The bike tips over; I'm dragged along the ground, leaving me scraped, bruised, and in considerable pain. Luckily, I don't hit my head, as I'm not wearing a helmet. A good Samaritan stops and calls the police on his cell phone. He speaks no English, but sits with me on the side of the road. A long scrape along my arm is bleeding. He goes to his truck and gets a bottle of water, which he pours over my wound. The policeman arrives, followed by an ambulance. No one speaks English, but they understand the words American and photographer as I mimic taking pictures. I write down my name on a form.

At the hospital, the doctor speaks basic English and gets a nurse to clean my wounds. My T-shirt is ripped, dirty and covered with blood. They take it and give me a hospital gown. They don't think I have any broken bones, but want me to get X-rays to be sure. A male nurse helps me hobble to a small building on the hospital grounds and deposits me in a plastic chair in an empty waiting room. He touches my strawberry hair and stares at me as if I were from another planet, his eyes like spots of coal framed by long, thick lashes. I try out the phrase I've learned for thank you, "*Teşekkür ederim.*" He smiles as he puts the paperwork in my hands and leaves.

From the other room, I hear a man and a woman talking. A child is crying. The cry turns to a wail, a desperate choking sound. The woman's words are agitated, the man's soothing. After a short time, the child is quiet. And later the woman in a hijab leaves the room carrying a small boy. The man calls out something in Turkish and I assume he is ready for me. He is sitting at a desk examining some papers. I notice his beautiful head of thick wavy hair and square jaw. He's wearing scrubs and glasses. I put the papers on his desk. He looks at them and then at me, startled. I'm still in the fog of pain and focus on the sweat soaking through the front and armpits of his top.

"Sorry. The air conditioning is kaput," he says in

excellent English. "And today of all days, the hottest day of the year." He stands up, takes off his glasses, and pulls the top of his scrubs over his head, hangs it on a hook. "I hope you don't mind. We are only men here now," he says, glancing at the door where the woman has just left.

I am delighted by the familiar face, the torso also unmistakable. I have gone through all my photos a dozen times and memorized the pattern of hair on his chest and the pleasure trail cascading down from his navel. I stare at the tiny jewels of sweat embedded in his chest hair. "Ibrahim," I croak.

He walks to his desk and looks at the papers again. "And you are Mr. Scott."

"Just Scott," I say. He takes my hand and holds it longer than a normal shake. He draws his hand away and touches his heart.

"You look so surprised. You think we *Pehlivan* have no life outside wrestling? We are not professionals. We must work."

He motions for me to sit on the examining table and goes behind me to untie the strings of my gown. "I remove this. I take X-rays, but first I want to see what I can see. Many times I don't need machines. I see or feel if there are broken bones. Please lie down. Oh, wait. Is better if you remove pants first."

"What?" I'm in a state of utter confusion, excitement mixed with bewilderment. I wouldn't normally be shy in front of a doctor, but I had photographed every inch of this man's exposed flesh, zoomed in on his face, and scoured every corner of the town in hopes of a glimpse of him.

He is amused by my hesitation. "Please," he says,

helping me undo my belt and sliding the pants down over my feet. When the fabric rubs my skinned knee and I wince with pain, he grimaces in sympathy.

I lie on the table in my underwear. He begins his examination, putting his warm hands on the sides of my head, letting his fingers burrow into my hair. His crotch is touching the top of my head. All I can think is, *Please, God, don't let me get a hard-on.*

His hands move down to my shoulders, gently moving over my skin, pressing lightly. "You are lucky," he says. "Your clavicles are fine. Very often, these are broken in this type of accident."

Next my arms. He covers inch by inch, kneading and prodding. I flinch when he gets near my arm wound. "Sorry," he says, moving to my ribs, touching them one by one. I'm ticklish and squirm. He laughs before moving to my upper thigh. I use every ounce of strength to control myself. I think of cold showers and a dead rat I once saw covered with maggots. It's no use; there's a stirring.

"Are you married?" he asks.

I wonder if this is a professional question. "No. Are you?"

"Not any longer."

"Divorced?"

"No. My wife died in childbirth."

"I'm sorry."

"I have a daughter." His eyes are misty with affection for her.

Though perplexed by this personal turn, I want to know everything about him. "Will you remarry?"

"Why?"

"I mean, for your daughter's sake."

"Are you making me a proposal?"

Now, this is weird. He can't say that. He knows I am enraptured, and he's playing with me. I try to laugh, but it hurts. "Ouch!" I say.

"In your country, this is possible for two men, no?"

I nod. There is a pounding under my ribs like a beast trying to get out.

He finishes his examination and lays a hand on my arm. "Good news, my friend. No broken bones. I won't do the X-rays." He has a peculiar smile on his face. "But I want to try something else."

Sweet Jesus! This is not happening. I have fantasized about this man since the moment I saw him. We are alone and my hard on rages inside my underwear.

"This maybe sounds a bit strange. Bear with me. Did you hear how rapidly the little boy stopped crying?"

"Yes, what did you do?"

"My grandma was a healer, gifted in the ancient ways. After my wrestling matches—I started when I was a boy—she would put me on a table and do the passing of hands. It would take away the pain. Before she died, she told me I have the gift. 'But,' I say, 'you tell me the gift is only passed down through the women of the family.' She shrugs and says, 'Times are changing.' I think this is not possible. I study modern medicine at the university here and then in Amsterdam to complete my studies. There I learn my English. I want to know nothing of the ancient ways and I'm embarrassed as a man my grandma thinks I have the gift. But sometimes, when people come to me in pain with broken bones, particularly children, I try the passing of hands. I find it works, that my grandma was right. So I want to try this for you."

I have reached my capacity for things I don't understand. "I'm good," I say. "I should go." I try to get up.

"Please," he says, putting a hand gently on my chest. "I only want to help."

In a few seconds, I am immobilized. Warmth spreads out from his fingers across my chest, up to my throat, down to my gut. My hard-on fades away, leaving only complete relaxation. I am sinking.

He puts his hands an inch or so above my solar plexus and slowly moves them to the top of my head, creating an aura of healing around me. By the third pass, I am out.

We are both in the stadium, now empty. The golden light of late afternoon surrounds us and falls on the grass, which still glistens with the oil and sweat from the wrestlers' bodies. The scent of grass tickles my nose, triggering my allergies, and my body arches in preparation for a gigantic sneeze. Ibrahim's hand instantly goes to my chest and the sneeze disappears.

Oil leaks out of his fingertips and he rubs it over my torso. It drips down. I worry it will stain my pants. At the same moment, I realize I wear no pants. I am naked, standing in the middle of the stadium where shortly before thousands of people had their eyes focused on this same spot. My next realization is he is naked, too, standing close, radiating warmth, his hands now on my shoulders. He puts one hand on the back of my head, pulling my lips to his. We are pressed together, his chest hair brushing my nipples. I no longer try to control my arousal and I feel him growing, too. He lifts me up, and in slow motion we tumble to the ground, the grass a cushion, a bed. We continue falling as if going to the center of the earth.

We roll over and over on the field, with blades of grass clinging to our bodies, now entwined in every position the wrestlers had previously assumed, wrapping arms, curling toes, sliding limbs, pressing flesh, not in battle but in a joining of bodies, of spirits. Tongues and lips explore. The taste of his skin is sweet and salty, with hints of oil. All boundaries have melted away. He is inside me and I in him at the same moment. Pressure mounts, bringing on our simultaneous explosions, our shouts of ecstasy echoing around the stadium. Aftershocks rock our bodies until we finally collapse into our joy and let our fluids— saliva, sweat, oil, semen—spill and drip onto the grass.

The sky turns rosy and the light falls away. We are looking up at the purple clouds, his arm under the back of my head. I hear his voice, but his lips don't move. "It will be with us forever." I don't understand his words. I am crying.

I open my eyes. My cheeks are wet. What I'm lying on is hard, not soft like the grass. The room is dark. I don't know where I am. I reach down and feel my damp underwear. I start to get up. "Slowly," a voice says.

I remember the accident, the radiologist, the passing of hands. I sit up on the edge of the table. "I was in another place."

"I know."

"You were there, too."

"Of course."

"I mean really there."

"I know." He turns on a low light and comes over to stand in front of me, a knowing expression on his face. On his right bicep, I see something, a dark streak that appears to be a blade of grass. I reach for it. It vanishes. My hand recoils.

"I have to go," I say. I stand up and look around the room for my pants. He puts his hands on my shoulders like he did in the dream or trance or whatever dark spell he put on me.

He pulls me into an embrace. My body stiffens. He whispers in my ear, "It will be with us forever."

"I don't know what that means," I whisper back.

"We don't have to understand everything, like my grandma said." He pulls back and looks deeply into my eyes. With his thumb, he brushes away a tear. I feel his power over me. "You have no reason to fear me, Scott."

"With this gift...can you...can you take people to another place...and do things?" I say.

"Only if both want it."

"Oh."

"How is your pain, my friend?"

It is only at this moment I realize my pain is gone. I am grateful and filled with awe, but still unsure of what to think, caught in the twilight between reality and fantasy.

"I have no more patients and tonight I must go to my daughter. But first I take you back to your hotel, make sure you are comfortably in bed."

"It's not necessary." I pull away from him and put on my pants.

"Oh my beautiful red apple, you have traveled across oceans to a country and language you do not know, and you're afraid to go one step further?"

I don't know whether to run or weep.

"Take my hand," he says. "It is as simple as a blade of grass."

# We *Are* the Revolution

The sea breeze carried the voice, gritty with salt, through the shuttered balcony doors and into the dim, musty sweatbox of a room. Jayden had for some time been listening to it, staring up at the whirling blades of the ceiling fan while the dead weight of a sleeping body half covered him, its head of thick black hair nestled into the crook of his arm. A pool of the sleeper's saliva gathered on his chest and a layer of sweat was painted along the seam where their bodies were stuck together.

The voice rose and fell with the shifting wind, but the fury was constant, at times climbing up to peaks where it was crowned with *revolución* or *socialismo*. Crackling with age though still full of fight, the source of the voice was unmistakable, and Jayden was shaken by the sting of the words aimed at *los imperialistas* of his native land. The barbs came, riding the dense air, from the square packed with a crowd a million strong into their little bedroom of two. The previous afternoon, he and Pedro had meandered through the extensive plaza, the Tribuna Antimperialista Jose Martí, where workmen put on the final touches for the demonstration.

The chilling erector-set construction of towers and arches delineated the stretch of concrete where anti-

American demonstrations had become a regular event since Elian Gonzalez had been plucked from an inner tube in the Straits of Florida and become a cause célèbre of the Miami Cuban community. The expanse of cement, the bare metal arches and stark stage at one end of the plaza were fitting companions to the building across the street, the concrete and glass, nine-story U.S. Interests Section, a non-embassy flaunting the lack of formal relations between the two neighboring countries in the midst of a fifty-year feud. The Goliath building and the Tribuna representing the island David sneer at each other across a no-man's-land forest of gigantic gunmetal flagpoles sporting black flags to commemorate the martyrs of the Revolution.

The voice reached a shaky but fervent pitch, sending the throng into an extended roar. Pedro sucked back a swallow of spit, wiped his mouth and rolled over on his side with a groan. Freed from his burden, Jayden got up, and went to look out the weathered wooden slats to the street one story below. Even this far from the square, an overflow crowd filled the street with a sea of red shirts and miniature, plastic, red, white and blue flags. Pedro's red shirt with the government factory logo over the left breast pocket lay forsaken on a chair in the corner, still wrapped in plastic. He had brought it home the previous evening and thrown it across the room, saying they had been ordered to attend the rally wearing it.

"They don't even let me sleep," moaned Pedro, stretching his torso and turning over to look at Jayden.

"That's the idea. You're supposed to be out there. You got the day off."

"For me, that's all it is, or was supposed to be. A day off. But you had to go and rent an apartment right next to demo central."

Jayden didn't mind Pedro went against the grain and might even say it excited him, but he knew life would be a lot easier if Pedro played the game a bit more. In the two weeks since they met, the police had stopped them four times. They questioned Pedro about being with a foreigner, and if he had flashed a party membership card or at least brought himself to wipe the annoyed look off his face and address the officers as *compañero,* things might have gone a lot smoother. The last time, to Jayden's horror and weak protest, the police had put Pedro in handcuffs and hauled him off to the central police station on Dragones. Jayden had followed in a taxi and stood outside because they wouldn't let him in. Pedro was out in thirty minutes, wearing a sneer that could have cooked an egg and holding a rough paper crumpled in his hand indicating a hefty fine for not respecting the officers. He threw it on the ground, but Jayden picked it up and glanced over his shoulder.

Pedro had a stack of fines his mother had informed Jayden with a weary smile, a hint of pride behind the lament she would be the one to pay them or get a lawyer to reverse them. The latest fine was on top of the one he got the week before for missing three days of work, sleeping in with Jayden those mornings rather than crawling out of bed at 6:00 a.m. like he was supposed to.

Their fledgling romance had been an every night thing since Jayden dragged him home from the Malecón like a door prize one evening after they both had had too much to drink. They had passed out, missing the chance to explore each other's bodies. Jayden awoke with the worry he had done something stupid. You don't drag someone home in a foreign country that you don't know anything about. But the worry promptly dissipated when the morning turned into a fiesta of skin on skin. And now every night was a marathon of pounding, shuddering sex followed by the soothing embrace of satisfied arms, the best sex he had ever had.

Leaning his bare back up against the rough door frame, Jayden gaped at Pedro, taking in his sleep-puffy face, his hair ruffled up in several directions, his hairy leg sticking out from under the sheet, and his thick-fingered laborer's hand absentmindedly caressing the bulge between his legs. Pedro stared back at the American, scanning his nakedness through the slits of his eyes still in rebellion against the morning light. A froggy voice emerged from his throat.

"Tell me what you see out there."

"I see a small girl with her hair in cornrows and her face smudged with vanilla ice cream. I see a big Black hand wrapped around a beer can. I see guilt in the eyes of an old woman, who like a bad puppy, has strayed from the voice. I see a teenage boy with his long skinny arm draped over a petite girl's shoulders, whispering something in her ear. It looks like a party. And every damn one of them is wearing a red shirt."

"Must look like blood flowing in the streets. It's the plague of Moses." He made the sign for beard to show he wasn't talking about Moses, but the man. "Come over here," he continued, trying to sound tough.

"Uh-uh," Jayden answered with a laugh.

Like a cat Pedro leaped out of the bed and was pressed against him in a second. He twisted Jayden's body around so that he enveloped him from behind in a tight embrace. Jayden gazed at the arm draped like a white stripe across his brown belly and laughed to himself at the reverse dynamic of the typical foreigner-Cuban relationship. He was the dark-skinned, funky-haired, big-lipped African-American and he got himself a green-eyed, pale-skinned, hunky white Cuban boy who insisted on calling him a mulatto. When Jayden first heard Pedro call him *mulatíco*, he was insulted. He was proud of his Blackness even though technically he was half white. That was before he learned there was this weird-shit Cuban thing about mulattos, not too white and not too dark, being on the top of the pyramid—at least as far as sexual desirability.

"Come on, baby," Pedro said in steamy puffs right into his ear, sending shivers all the way down to his toes. "We got our own baby revolution going here. Let's make it happen."

"God, do you ever get enough. I'm already late. Aisha and I've got a lot of work to do."

"You mean that Black bitch isn't out there drooling over her hero?"

Jayden cringed and tried to wriggle out of Pedro's embrace. "I hate it when you say shit like that. You think you're funny, but you're a racist. What are you doing with me?"

Pedro tightened his grip. "*Tranquilo*, baby. Just joking. Anyway, I'm sure she says worse things about me. I know she hates me."

"She doesn't hate you, but she doesn't appreciate you thumbing your nose at the revolution. This country took her in and gave her a life. They saved her from being murdered or rotting away in prison the rest of her days."

"I know. You told me. But that's the point. She's not a real Cuban and doesn't have to live like we live. She's taken care of."

Jayden's cell phone rang and Pedro let him escape.

"You better get your Black ass out here 'cause I been waiting a half hour already. You're missing the whole thing. I know what your excuse is and I don't even want to hear it," Aisha bellowed over the line. Even though she had been out of the States for over twenty-five years, she was still an east coast city girl with a mouth.

"You sound like my mama. Matter of fact, we were having a political discussion. And as far as missing everything, we're practically in the middle of it. We can hear every word."

Aisha Kintu was the other Black Panther who fled to Cuba during the mid-seventies crackdown on the Black Power movement. Both Assata Shakur and William Lee Brent had told their stories of exile in Cuba, but Aisha had kept a low profile until one day she decided it was time to tell hers. Jayden's boss at *Rolling Stone* had sent him down to Havana to write a piece on her.

Jayden and Aisha had hit it off from the start. The woman, about the same age as Jayden's mother, had chosen the Black Panthers, while Jayden's mother, though sympathetic to the cause, had chosen a comfortable life when she married a white doctor from New Orleans, already pregnant, a double scandal. Jayden sometimes regretted the banality of his middle-class upbringing and loved the afternoon sessions with Aisha, where they would set down in words the intrigue, adventure, and sacrifices of her life.

As Jayden pulled on his faded and shredded jeans, he glanced at Pedro's naked body sprawled on top of the sheets, feeling a growing regret Pedro had given up trying to seduce him and gone back to sleep. A boyfriend hadn't been part of the plan. Jayden had come here to work, and he only had two weeks left to finish the article. With no possibility it would be done, he was already contemplating asking Lucila for an extension. She would scream about going over budget. Let her. It wasn't his fault each time they got together Aisha kept spewing out information, and a minute later retracting it because she wasn't sure she should tell a particular story. He pulled a T-shirt over his head, thinking about all the things he and Pedro might do with the extra time.

★

A pang of loneliness struck Jayden as soon as he opened the door after his editing session with Aisha, and it was punctuated by the clank of his keys crashing onto the glass-topped table, ringing throughout the empty rooms. Pedro was out. No note. No phone call. Jayden booted up his laptop and sat down to read through the part he and Aisha had gone over that afternoon.

*When we left the gathering to go back to the apartment, Bobby gave me a gun. It felt heavy and cold in my hand. "What am I supposed to do with this? I never even fired one before." We all knew NYPD had busted down the door of one of our houses a few days before. Sweet Sue and Paco had been shot. I got an icy feeling running up and down my body. What if I had to shoot somebody, kill somebody? I wasn't raised to do that. But I was raised to stand up for myself. My mama didn't want me to go through what she had, working her fingers to the bone, cleaning for some white folks. She sent me to Hunter College and I was a good student. My major was political science, but it felt academic and bourgeois to be sitting in the library when there was a revolution going on outside.*

Jayden had one run-in with the police, driving home with friends from a Tina Turner concert in his father's BMW. Several of them had afros and the cops assumed it was a stolen car, soon had them spread eagle against the beamer, conducting a search complete with racist verbal abuse. None of them protested as they were all good uptown boys, and they were let go when his father verified ownership of the car. The anger and shame of that night remained a splinter in his soul. He had done nothing, had put up with the harassment. Kept his mouth shut. Aisha wouldn't have done that.

Darkness fell on the room only lit by the cool blue glow from the screen. He got up to turn on a light, and at the same moment his phone began a vibrating dance on the table.

"Are you decent?" It was Aisha.

"Decent and alone."

"Poor baby. I'll pick you up in forty-five minutes. Wear something nice."

★

He slammed the door of the banged-up, second-hand Lada, making Aisha wince at the door's tinny rattle. Cars were hard to come by and she was lucky to have it, such as it was. "OK, mystery lady. Where we going?" he asked.

"A small gathering."

"Come on. Tell me."

"You'll find out soon enough." She had a smile about as wide as the windshield and she kept taking big gulps of air and letting it out.

"Don't play coy with me, girl. Something's going on."

She kept nodding, about to burst.

"All right, you know the group of writers and artists from Harlem here in Havana? He invited me to a dinner with them and I asked if I could bring a friend. I told you were a Marti scholar." Jayden had written his master's thesis on Jose Marti.

"He who? No. No way. You *are* shitting me. No. Turn this car around."

"What's the matter with you? This is a chance in a lifetime, honey. And you owe it all to me."

"I can't go in there."

"And why the hell not?"

"Them's communists. Don't they eat gay boys for breakfast? They'll probably ship me off to a concentration camp."

"Oh, they haven't done that in thirty years."

"Eat gay boys for breakfast or ship them off to concentration camps?"

"Not exactly a concentration camp. More a re-education center. That was a long time ago. These days things are different. You don't even want to know how many closet cases there are in the government...at the highest levels. I say no more."

"You mean I might get a date?"

"I thought you were taken."

"Oh, yeah. I almost forgot, my racist boyfriend."

The pat down and distrustful eyes of the guard at the door made Jayden anxious, but once they were inside the banquet room, he relaxed and let his gaze wander around the hall with its marble walls and heavy brown drapes lining one wall at the far end. The décor was hideous. "Gays in the government?" he said out loud. "Coulda fooled me."

"Shush yo mouth," said Aisha.

The ten round tables set up on the floor were covered with beige tablecloths and each one had a bottle of Havana Club rum as the centerpiece. For the dignitaries there was a long table on a raised platform at the head of the room, set apart by a surprisingly shabby pale gold cloth. Seated at the center of the table, an old man leaned over to talk to a middle-aged woman, making her giggle and blush. It was him. Jayden stood transfixed in the middle of the room, astounded by the man's frailness.

Aisha grabbed his arm and steered him to their table. "You're gawking," she said.

"Oh my God. Wait till I tell Lucila."

As Jayden eased into the chair—their table was right at the foot of the stairs that led up to the podium—he caught the eye of the woman sitting next to the man and gave her his most winning smile as if sharing her glory at sitting next to the room's focal point. He had always tried to be logical in his approach to the Castro question, as he was to most everything in his life—his affair with Pedro aside. Sex had a way of scrapping your best-laid plans. He had recently read Fidel's words in *To Speak the Truth,* a collected work of Fidel and Che Guevara's speeches, and a lot of it made sense. But he also saw the man as somewhat of an egomaniac, and what he had witnessed on the streets of Cuba didn't exactly look like a success story. Now, in his presence, he found himself gushing like everyone else in the room.

As soon as they sat down, Aisha reached for the bottle of Havana Club—already half gone—and poured shots for her and Jayden. Part of the Harlem delegation was sitting at their table, and Aisha initiated a conversation with a poet who was anxious to meet her. Only half listening to the mix of English and Spanish at his table, Jayden kept one ear tuned to the heavily accented English coming from the main table. The dark-skinned woman with the big copper hair getting all the man's attention was the leader of the Harlem delegation. He had seen her on the news when they arrived at the airport. With his back to the platform, he leaned back trying to eavesdrop on what they were saying. Aisha gave him an eye of caution he was being obvious, and then said in a low voice, "Most people don't know he speaks English quite well though he doesn't do it publicly. I don't suppose a lot of the New York group speak Spanish."

"Can I trade places with you? I can't see," he hissed.

"No. No more gawking."

While the man was seated, he exuded charm and power, commanding the room without lifting a finger. But when he rose to speak, the full effect of his signature army fatigues came into view and a hush fell over the room. He was amusing and defiant, clever and sane, forthcoming and mysterious. He talked of his visits to Harlem, baseball, the medical scholarships, Marti, the importance of literature and art, and joked about being the old goat in the new world order. After a mere half hour, his speech came to an abrupt end, and he apologized state matters were taking him away from this finest of gatherings where intellect and heart and the tenets of the revolution all came together.

Amid the standing ovation from the crowd, he started down the three steps to the main floor. A man from the other side of the platform said something to him and he turned just as his boot caught the edge of the first step, and for an endless second he was teetering on the brink of a fall. Most of the room didn't see it, but everyone at Jayden's table gasped. He was down before anyone could move. Jayden knocked over his chair, upsetting several water glasses, as he reached out and caught an arm that was thrown out to break the fall, but one knee had already scraped against the bottom step and the other cracked against the floor. With the man's arm locked in his, Jayden threw the other around his waist and lifted him without the slightest concern for what he was doing. Half standing, Fidel had a vice grip on Jayden's bicep and they were eye to eye. Jayden noted the pain, but what most impressed him were the soft eyes, not hard like he had imagined.

"*Gracias, joven,*" the man said, fighting through his agony. Jayden moved him toward a chair. He peered over Jayden's shoulder at Aisha. "You must be the Marti scholar."

"*Sí, señor.*"

"Not sir. *Campañero,*" he said in English with a pained laugh. "Say, what did Marti write about growing old?"

"Not much, I suppose. He died at 42."

"You are wrong. He is alive. In everything we do here, in every day of our lives, he is alive." The man smiled and Jayden stared at his stained teeth, the age spots on his face and the scraggly hairs of his beard.

In the small world of this moment, Jayden was holding up history, touching something much bigger than a frail old man. The rush in his bloodstream was strangely like being on ecstasy. And then, in a cruel instant, he was catapulted back onto the floor as the man's astounded eyes faded into a sea of security guards. A guard who had the girth of a football player was on top of him, holding his arms against the floor above his head. People were screaming and walkie-talkies were crackling high code alerts. Aisha tried to explain Jayden didn't do anything, that it was an accident and he had only wanted to help. Another guard pushed her away and she fell back into a chair.

"*Qué haces? Es mi amiga*. What the hell?" said Jayden in his new mode of trying to stand up to abuse.

"*Callate*," he said before slamming Jayden across the face to shut him up.

Over the din, Jayden heard the voice. "*Dejalo en paz. No hizo nada.*" When they carried the leader away on a stretcher, he tried to look back, but there were too many people in between for Jayden to have one last look into those soft eyes.

★

Pedro held Jayden in his arms and kissed the spot still stinging from the cuff on the jaw. Then he slid his tongue down into Jayden's ear.

"You bastard, I can't do anything. I'm too sore. That big ape was rough."

Pedro smirked. "You like it rough. Bet you even got a hard on."

"Shut up. You know there ain't nobody but you."

"Uh-huh." Pedro slid his hand down into Jayden's pants. "Anyway, our own little revolution needs to be fed like anything else. Why do you go looking for something out there? It's here. It's us."

"Revolution you call it? We're simply filling our needs. If anything, it sometimes feels like you're taking it out on me, pounding into me your frustration with things you can't have, like you're saying 'Fuck you America' for keeping Fidel in power through its stupid-assed policies, which pretend to be doing the opposite."

"Anytime you want to stop, let me know."

A light rain tapped the corrugated plastic roof next door. The air in the room was damp and getting heavier. He made one last attempt at resistance. "Stop. I'm serious."

Pedro moved his hand around in Jayden's shorts. "I can feel exactly how serious you are."

They kissed and Jayden let his body go, but in his head he still heard the voice and pictured those eyes, lamenting he didn't have a better answer about what Marti would say about growing old.

# All in the Cuban Family

The Ocho Vias highway stretches out in front of me like a giant landing strip—flat, wide and almost empty. At various points there are hints of lane markings, so you can actually count the eight lanes, but most of the line paint has been worn down to speckles, distant fading constellations. I guess where I am supposed to drive, though there is so little traffic it hardly matters.

It has turned surprisingly warm for January and the sun has reached the peak of its winter arc, beating down on the lonely pavement in front of my Toyota Yaris, a small 4-door coupe I rented an hour before. The car cruises well at eighty miles per hour and if the freeway went all the way to Holguin, I could be there in about six hours. Later I look at the map and confirm what the rental agent told me, the construction of this magnificent stripe down the backbone of the island was stunted years before and only extends a little past Sancti Spiritus, halfway to my destination.

I am alone in the car, and for long stretches I don't see another vehicle. I listen to Trio Los Panchos—old cassettes borrowed from a friend in Havana—harmonizing their way through heartbreak after heartbreak. They have a way of glorifying the tragedy of love and it makes me feel my journey is both futile and inevitable. At the last minute I pulled out of the trip Leo and I had planned together, spoiling the New Year's celebration. Now guilt pulls me along and lends weight to my gas pedal foot while the melodies and soulful plucking of the Trio's guitar strings churn up restless emotions. I shudder with ridiculous emotions as I wipe a tiny tear from the corner of my eye.

The countryside is vibrant green, dotted by tall, skinny palms shaking their fronds at the powdery sky. I turn off the music and let myself sink into the tranquil scenery, letting the first few hours fly by like a meditation—my eyes fixed on the blankness of the road, my position frozen with a singleness of purpose. Soon the wide road ends and I find myself on the two-lane Carretera Central that drops me off in the middle of towns and dares me to find my way to the other side; signage is poor or nonexistent. On the outskirts of each town, I fight for road space with trucks, cars, horse-drawn carriages, tractors, bicycles, motorcycles, motorcycles with sidecars, and pedestrians. To further distract me are people at every intersection flagging down rides, many of them coming out into the road and waving peso bills to show that they are willing to pay.

The first time I stop to pick up riders is in Ciego de Avila. I am lost. I followed the first two signs, but I have driven through a good part of the town without seeing another one. A young couple with a baby stares longingly into my car when I am stopped at the sole traffic light in town and I wave for them to get in. The young man gets in the front and his petite wife and young baby get in the back. They mumble, "*Gracias*," but say no more. The dad is as slender as the newly planted saplings on the side of the road, about twenty-five years old, and is wearing faded jeans and worn-out sneakers. It is all I can do to stop myself from laying my hand on his bony knee and reassuring him that he will get home all right. He stares straight ahead stoically, so I turn my attention to the mother in the back, smiling at her through the rear view mirror. I figure it is acceptable since I am, in fact, smiling at the baby. She holds my gaze a second before looking down at the bundle in her arms. I imagine they could be Leo and his little family.

"I'm lost," I announce. "Can you direct me back to the highway to Camaguey? I hope that is the way you are going."

"Oh, yes," says the young man in the clipped, scratchy Spanish that tells me we are getting into Eastern Cuba. "No problem. I can tell you. We are going to Florida."

"Oh, really? Miami?" I joke.

"No, our city is Florida, here in Cuba," the man says with a firm jaw.

"Yes," says the woman, in an equal deadpan. "Florida, Cuba."

The conversation doesn't pick up much from there. I ask about the baby. She is three months old and her name is Mayalin. They have been to visit the woman's father in Ciego de Avila, who saw the baby for the first time. They don't ask me any questions, but I tell them my name is Martin and that I am from Los Angeles...California, USA. They remain expressionless and we fall silent.

Soon we escape the jam and jumble of the city and though we are on the open road, it doesn't mean we are moving fast. There are still the horse-drawn taxis and tractors slowing traffic and making it impossible to pass. When we get to Florida, I pull over and the family slips out of the car like ghosts. Their parting words are, "Go straight," and I stay the course through the town, miraculously finding myself on the road out in the direction of Camaguey. A few minutes later I wonder if I imagined the whole incident.

About an hour outside of Holguin, I get Leo on the phone and we exchange tentative hellos. I inform him I'm only an hour away,

"Martin, you're crazy." He says it softly, as though he is pleased, but still reluctant to say it. "When you get into town, ask people how to get to the Carretera de Gibara. Everybody knows where it is. Look for me on the side of the road near the clinic."

It sounds like the typical Cuban plan that has heart, but is short on substance, leading to crossed paths, but in fact it works. The first people I stop give me good directions and soon I am on a road I recognize from my trip to Holguin one and a half years before. The usual mishmash of vehicles and pedestrians keeps the traffic moving slowly, so I have no trouble spotting Leo walking in my direction with a slight limp like a cowboy who has recently fallen off a horse.

I pull over and he gets into the car with his freshly showered scent and shiny damp hair, so black some strands look blue. We do one of those always-unsatisfying driver to passenger hugs, and then I get back on the road. I look over and see the beguiling smile spreading across to his finely sculpted cheekbones, making him look all pleased with himself. He knows he got me again, and he knows I know he knows. Just being in the same car with him makes me feel I have some purpose in life. I put my hand on his leg and he slides his fingers in between mine. It is like the first night we met, and I'm racked by same crackling sensation. Once again, it is so easy to make up.

"You look fine to me," I say. "You didn't make this whole accident thing up so I would come and get you, did you?"

He turns his face and shows me a bruise under his eye on the right side and a cut on his forehead. "Most of what hurts is what you can't see."

"Your aching heart from missing me so bad? Or do you mean down here?" I say, slipping my hand onto his crotch.

"No," he gasps modestly and squirms, looking out the window to see who might be watching. "I mean I'm kind of sore all over. Anyway, I didn't ask you to come."

"I know, but now that I'm here I'll see what I can do to make you feel better."

"I already feel better being with you," he says quietly, almost embarrassed.

We turn into his gravelly, potholed street and he puts a hand on my arm. "Wait, let me drive."

I stop the car and let him take the driver's seat, knowing it is a boon for him to be seen driving a new car down his street. We proceed at a snail's pace past the crude, unfinished dwellings. To several people trudging along the dusty road he waves almost imperceptibly, as if this were an everyday occurrence. In the soft luminosity of twilight, the houses from which these downtrodden souls emerge look picturesque but minimal protection from the elements, as if a big storm might lay the place to shambles.

He stops in front of a dreary-looking house with a corrugated plastic roof, turns the car off and gets out. "Come on," he says.

We climb the bare steps, and Leo pushes aside a dingy curtain. Inside are several women sitting wide-eyed on a few mismatched rusty chairs under a bare bulb that hangs precariously from the ceiling on unraveling cords. The brick walls are exposed and not for a trendy effect. Leo introduces me to a small, thin, pretty woman who is holding a tiny thing wrapped in a blanket.

I have barely gotten into town and I am face to face with the stark reality of his life. Here is the woman, Sulyn, and his daughter, Anabela. I try not to act shocked. I kiss Sulyn on the cheek and coo at the baby, whose eyes are pressed shut in a grimace. There is a smell of fried onions hanging in the air. He introduces me to Sulyn's sister, who I kiss dutifully, and then her mother, who gives me a hard, cold stare and sticks out a calloused hand.

"Well, let's go," Leo says to Sulyn. She follows.

I offer Sulyn and the baby the front seat, but she waves me off as if I am being ridiculous and meekly crawls in the back.

We drive the two blocks to Leo's house and his mom, Lisbeth, rushes out when she hears the car pull up. She hugs and kisses me, but calls me "*Sin Vergüenza.* Shameless."

"I'm still mad at you," she warns. "You should have been here for New Year's. All the family was here except you."

I don't know how to respond. She is both honoring me, by calling me part of the family, and chastising me.

"Well, I'm here now," I blurt out uncomfortably.

Inside the house I finally get to see the baby. I notice she is *not* wearing any of the outfits I have sent with Leo. She has woken up and is looking around with a distinctly curious expression.

"Do you want to hold her?" says Leo. He puts her in my arms. She weighs almost nothing, but her face seems ancient and wise. It is obvious that she has her father's deep brown eyes and luscious mouth, and a wisp of dark hair that stands straight up. I make silly faces at her, and after a look of consternation, she begins to react.

"Look," says Lisbeth. "She smiled at her...uh...*tio*." Everybody laughs. As she grows up, will she call me Uncle? Never Dad?

The small living room is full of family—Leo's grandmother, aunt, and several cousins. They are crowded around the little princess and heaping smiles on me. Sulyn has disappeared into Lisbeth's bedroom.

Leo and I sit down to eat dinner. He invites Sulyn to join us, but she says no. She has reappeared and is holding the baby over in a corner of the room. Lisbeth loads food on our plates and warns me I had better eat. Since I ate little on the road, I have a good appetite, but I still feel overwhelmed, wondering if I can do justice to the huge plate she has put before me. Leo is beaming like the king of the mountain surrounded by his loyal subjects, and despite the unlikelihood of my presence in the gathering, I get caught up in his light.

When we finish, I carry plates into the kitchen and

Lisbeth corrals me between the sink and the refrigerator. "I'm worried about that car," she tells me in a low voice. "You've got to help him. If the owners don't think he can pay for the damage, they might come after him." The car he drove to Holguin, and the one I was supposed to come in, was a private rental with a handshake agreement. Now it's a wreck.

"I don't know. I haven't even talked to him about it yet."

"After all, none of this would have happened if you had come with him."

She has left me speechless twice in less than an hour. So it is all my fault. "Look, Lisbeth. My decision not to come in that car was completely justified. He shouldn't have contracted that piece of junk without consulting me first."

"But..."

I hold up my hand. "Wait. Of course I'm not going to let Leo get into trouble. We'll work something out. At the same time, he has to take some of the responsibility. I still don't know what happened."

Leo comes into the kitchen and gives us a funny look. "What are you two talking about?"

"I have some things I need to discuss with Martin. Nothing for you to worry about."

"We need to go to the place I called about renting a room. Anyway, I'm sure he's tired. You can talk tomorrow."

"I thought we were going to the beach tomorrow," says Lisbeth.

He lets out an impatient groan. "You can talk at the

beach then."

On the way to the rental place, he tells me what happened with the car. The day after they arrived from Havana, he took the car over to show Pedro, a mechanic friend of his. The man fiddled with the carburetor, changed the oil, and put air in the tires. He said he wouldn't charge anything except for the oil, but he needed a big favor. His father, who was sick and might not live much longer, lived in the small town of Banes about forty-five minutes from Holguin. He needed the car to go see him for New Year's. It was a real sob story and of course Leo fell for it. He loves to help people out, so they agreed to meet at a bar on the edge of town later that afternoon. When Leo got there, the mechanic and his friend invited him to have a drink. They had several, and he didn't know how many they'd had before he even got there.

The plan was for them to drop Leo off, and later Pedro and his friend would go on to visit his father. Pedro insisted on driving and his companion was in the passenger seat while Leo sat in back. As soon as they were on the road, Leo realized his mistake. Pedro was drunk and driving recklessly.

"I can't let you take this car. You're stinking drunk," said Leo.

"But you promised." Pedro turned around and glared at Leo in the back seat. "You can't change your mind now, *maricon.*"

"Hey! Watch where you're going!" said his friend. A car honked and Pedro swerved back into his lane.

Leo yelled at him to stop the car and get out because they weren't going anywhere. An argument ensued and the driver took his eyes off the road again, turning around to shout at Leo in the back seat.

"I couldn't believe it," says Leo. "One second I was looking at his ugly mug and the next I was upside down, the car turning over and over. It was like something you see in the movies. I guess we went off the road where there was a steep embankment. The car flipped over two times and landed on the roof. The windows were all smashed, so it was easy to crawl out. I was bleeding from a cut on my head, but we were all right for the most part."

"God protects drunks and babies," I say. "I'm not even going to mention how stupid that was."

"Don't rub it in. I know it. But you should have seen that asshole. He had his fat self there on the ground sitting like a Buddha. He was blubbering and carrying on, saying he was sorry and all that shit."

"So is he going to pay for it?"

"With what? He doesn't have any money." I give him a disgusted look. "Don't be mad at me, baby. I'm sorry." He reaches over and starts stroking my leg. I don't want to be mad at him, and I am too tired anyway.

We get to the address, which turns out to be a fifties-era bungalow on the corner in a well-kept neighborhood. The owner, Roberto, is a short, skinny, likeable guy about my age. He lives in the house with his plump wife, his frail mother, and a teenage son. He is educated and has a good command of English.

He shows us the room, which has its own entrance and bathroom. It is spotless and simply decorated, and I immediately feel comfortable there. As we fill in the paperwork, Leo says he wants to be registered as the companion. Roberto gives him a doubtful look. "Are you planning on spending the night?"

"Well not tonight, but tomorrow I probably will."

"I want to make sure you don't mind being on record. I have to show my book to the local authorities, you know."

Leo scoffs as if he doesn't care what the government or anybody thinks. "I have nothing to hide."

"No problem. It's your call," says Roberto.

As soon as we are alone, he grabs me and plants his mouth on mine, and we kiss as though we are discovering each other for the first time. I squeeze him and he winces. "Whoa, boy. Remember the accident."

"Sorry. Get your clothes off and let me see."

We undress and he shows me his bruises, which I kiss one by one. He is beautiful, all of him, his scars, bruises and tattoos. I want to protect him, save him from his erratic life pointing toward a humdrum finale of regret. We lie down on the bed and continue kissing and touching in a skinfest. I am losing my head again, off in some fantasyland, drunk on his breath. It seems so right, so perfect. Yet another voice inside me says, "Suck it up. Get every last drop of this moment. Relish it. Wallow in it. Because tomorrow we might be on opposite sides of the country, the continent, the world."

We lie in the post sex stupor, neither one saying anything. My head is on his chest listening to his heart slowing down, and he is running his fingers through my fine hair. I open my eyes and realize the room has gone dark in another blackout. A motorcycle roars down the street as if opening a wound on the skin of the night before the darkness returns to silence, covering it up. Leo's hand stops and goes lax. After a few minutes, his body jerks, catching itself from falling. It is so dark I can't see his face, but I feel his smile.

"I'm falling asleep." He whines like a little kid. "I have to go."

"No you don't."

"Yes, I do."

"No you don't, damn it."

"Yes, I do, damn it."

It is useless to argue. I'm not going to win this one. He raises himself up and starts to dress.

★

Unlike the potholed Gibara road where I picked him up, the highway to the beach town of Guardalavaca is wide and well maintained. The Toyota flies along despite the heavy load—Leo at the helm, me as the co-pilot, Lisbeth, Lisbeth's boyfriend, Sulyn and the baby, and Leo's cousin, Adita. It is a perfect sunny day and quite warm. It is a day to feel optimistic and part of something.

We pass through the hilly countryside with sugarcane fields on either side and then down to the beach where groups of blond, pasty Canadians wrapped in colorful attire make their way to the seaside. They have just flown in by the planeload to take over the resorts of Guardalavaca, which are off limits to Americans.

Our little "family" descends the steps to the beach where spread out before us is the fine, sugary sand and many palm and sea grape trees offering shade. The water is aquamarine and broken only by gentle surf. We spread our towels out under the shiny leaves of a sea grape tree. Leo, with the ring I have given him on a gold chain bouncing against his chest, sets up his family close to the trunk of the tree where there is full shade while the rest of us spread out nearby where the sun shines through. Sulyn has a permanent scowl on her face, though Leo remains blind to everything except his daughter, cuddling Anabela in his arms and speaking to her in soft baby talk.

Nobody is interested in going in the water; it is warm, but for Cubans it is winter and the water is too cold. Lisbeth suggests she and I take a walk down the beach. As we head off, Leo looks up and squints in our direction, but hastily returns to cooing at the baby.

We walk along in silence for a few minutes. I slow my steps in order to not get ahead of her. Her Rubenesque body more than fills out the red one-piece bathing suit—she has asked me several times to bring her diet pills from the States—and her bundle of dark hair is tucked up under a red USMC baseball cap.

Finally she turns to me with beads of sweat on her forehead and says, "He's all I've got. He's my whole life." She speaks almost desperately and I am afraid I am going to get the "stay away from my son" speech.

"I know," I mutter.

"But there is no life for him here. He seems lost. One day he is selling soap on the black market and the next he is raising roosters for cockfights. I am constantly worried he is going to get into trouble."

"I wish he would focus more on his painting. I honestly think he has something there."

"Oh, I don't know. They are so dark. I wish he would

paint happier things."

"But that's why they are so good. He reaches down into his soul and expresses himself, not simply painting what people want to see. It's what art is all about."

"Well, you know about such things and I appreciate you trying to encourage him. I know he thinks a lot of you." I guess she can't bring herself to say the "love" word. "If he comes to live with you, all I ask is you take care of him. It would break my heart to see him go, but I know he needs to develop as a person. He has a lot of his father in him and if he stays here, he will end up like him."

Her words ring odd to me. "I never imagined you would want him to be with me...I mean especially after having a daughter and all that."

"I want him to be happy. I know he is not happy with Sulyn. She doesn't give him the support he needs. He is not always an easy person to be with, but he has a good heart."

"I know that. But what concerns me is he doesn't do his part as far as getting ready to leave. He needs to take some initiative. I'm not even sure he wants to go. I always thought he was reluctant because he felt bad for you, and he even implied you were against it. Now I am beginning to see the struggle is mostly within himself."

"I guess I have spoiled him. I always tried to give him everything I could, which wasn't much. But when he has to, he will work, and work hard. You are right, though. He struggles a lot with decisions and sometimes makes the wrong ones."

I want to point out that having a child at this stage of his life wasn't one of his brighter decisions, but as she is one of the main instigators of him becoming a father, I think it better not to bring it up.

"We all make some bad ones. But he needs to start thinking about what is good for his future, not only what is good for the moment."

"I think being a father has changed him little, forced him to grow up."

To be honest, I don't see it. He is loving and responsible in taking care of the baby, but it still seems to me a game for him, allowing him to postpone what he needs to do in his life. And I am not helping much by supporting him, allowing him to not face the harsh financial reality of being a new father. I can't tell her everything I am thinking, but I am content with the fact she is in a sense giving her blessing to our union.

At the end of the conversation, I can only promise I will do everything I can to take care of her son. Yet I am promising her something I don't even know if he wants anymore. Since our reunion we are stepping lightly around each other, and his leaving the country hasn't been brought up since that night in the rain when I refused to get in the car.

When Leo comes to pick me up that evening, I haven't showered yet. The sun sapped my strength and I crashed on the bed with the sand still in my trunks and between my toes. His knock on the door startles me.

He kisses me and slaps me on the butt. "Come on. They are waiting on us for dinner."

"Who? What?"

He rolls his eyes. "Wake up, sleepyhead. My mom fixed dinner for us. Then we're going out with my cousin and some friends. And guess what?"

"What?" Question words are all I can manage in my grogginess.

"We'll go out, but I'll come back and sleep here. I'll say I am too drunk to drive home." He hugs me excitedly, thrilled with his cleverness.

"And Sulyn?" I ask.

"No way. She's not going. She doesn't even like to go out."

On the way to his mother's house we stop and pick up Sulyn and the baby. I stay in the car, and when they come out, the unrest is evident in each step. Leo grimaces as he starts the car and Sulyn looks rather dressed up for a simple night at home.

As soon as we get in the house, Leo and Sulyn take the baby into Lisbeth's room and everybody can hear them arguing. The atmosphere worsens around the dinner table spread with plates of chicken and onions, rice, beans, salad and malanga. Lisbeth sighs and looks nervously at Leo as she sets the dishes down on the table. Sulyn is again off in a corner with the baby on her lap, and this time with a half-smile on her lips.

While we are eating, a young couple saunters in and Leo introduces me to his cousin Yordani, and his girlfriend, Daniela. Leo had told me about her, an ex-girlfriend his mother had disapproved of. Later we all get in Yordani's car, leaving Lisbeth holding the baby. She takes Anabela's hand and wags it to say goodbye. I look at Leo and he shrugs as though there is nothing he can do. It means Leo will be dropping me off at the end of the night and I'll be sleeping alone.

I get my first taste of what being out in public with my boyfriend and his wife is like when we get to Parque Calixto Garcia. The park draws a crowd every night and it takes us a while to find enough bench space where the five of us can sit down. Leo sits with Sulyn on one end, then Yordani and Daniela in the middle, and I am at the other end, far away from Leo. I try not to gawk, but it is hard not to notice Leo's arm around her, and her hand on his leg. I know the night could easily turn into a disaster if I show any signs of jealousy, so I try to reel in my feelings on a line that barely holds the weight. I ask Yordani for a cigarette and smoke for the first time in front of Leo. It gets his attention, and he leans forward to glare at me. "*Que haces?*"

In the Pico Cristal discothèque on the corner of the square, we get a bottle of rum and some Coke to mix Cuba Libres. The DJ spins dance music, starting with the ubiquitous Reggaeton. It has become the music of choice wherever young people congregate and seems to fit well with the bump and grind sexuality of Cubans. Leo is dancing with a group while Sulyn sits at the table with her head slightly bowed, not talking to anyone, her back to the dance floor. He motions for me to join them and I give her a wry smile as I shuffle past.

On the floor, Leo asks, "How's it going?"

I give him an unenthusiastic, "Okay."

He tilts his head and grants me his sweet-as-pie look. "Come on. There's nothing I can do about it." We are bobbing up and down, leaning close together as we talk.

Most of the others in the group have drifted away, so it looks as if we are dancing as a couple. I feel uneasy about being the only male-male couple on the dance floor. Leo is oblivious, smiling, looking at me with vacant adoration.

"Nothing?"

"She insisted on coming. I tried to talk her out of it. In a few days we'll be back in Havana and everything will be back to normal."

I nod though I am amused that "normal" means us being together. I feel a smile loosening my face as the music pumps "*La batidora, la batidora…*" The rum lets me enjoy the absurdity of life, the uncommon destinations when taking the road less traveled.

★

We stay one more day in Holguin before driving back to Havana through the night with Leo doing the major part of the driving. I only have three days left in Cuba and we sleep most of the first one. Leo never managed to spend the night with me in Holguin, so when we finally get into bed together, we get so tangled up in each other's limbs it is hard to tell where one body starts and the other ends.

We are on the seventh floor of a building on Primera with a balcony overlooking the sea. We get up late in the afternoon and watch one of the most beautiful sunsets I have ever seen from the two metal rocking chairs on the balcony. As the sun touches the horizon, we listen to Luis Miguel. The combination of his voice, the bleeding pastels of sundown, and my upcoming departure stir up an emotional cauldron.

We look at each other and Leo jerks his head toward

the black fake-leather sofa just inside the living room. Still with a prime view of the fading light, we make sweaty love, our bare skin squeaking and sticking to the plastic. We laugh, and then hurtle out our groans to the fading light before peeling ourselves off the sofa to go clean up.

The next couple of days pass much too rapidly, and before I've had a chance to prepare myself for the separation, I am crawling into a taxi at dawn to catch a morning flight. Leo is with me, but says he doesn't want to go to the airport. "Too sad," he says. I drop him off at a friend's. I get out of the taxi to say goodbye and he indicates for me to carry one of his bags up to the porch. The chill of tropical winter is in the air and I wish I had a jacket instead of only a long-sleeved shirt. Up on the porch, surrounded by plants and semi-darkness, we drop the bags and hold each other tightly. Our lips meet in the bittersweet kisses of goodbye as early morning birds belt out their songs. I tear myself away, carefully descending the broken steps in the shadow of my already emerging loneliness. I don't look back as I get in the taxi and slump into the silence of the back seat. On this trip, I have seen my Cuban family grow and then get smaller. Soon I will be alone.

# Market Day in Qatif

The bus rattled and swayed along the straight, smooth highway, rushing through the pale wind-swept sands to the oasis ahead. Fertile smells with a hint of dampness drifted in the windows, telling us we were nearing Qatif, site of the biggest market in the area. On either side of the highway, workers with scarves wrapped around their heads and baggy pants rolled up to their knees waded through the rows of tomatoes, okra, radishes, and onions, while clusters of date palms lingered in the distance as if overseeing their work.

I had set out that morning in a state of despair, and on the brink of quitting my job and leaving the Kingdom. It had been a horrendous week and an escape, an adventure, could be the answer to maintain my sanity.

On Monday, two of the students at the Royal Saudi Naval Base where I taught got into a fight, escalating from verbal insults to shoving. I sent one of the other cadets to get an officer as we were instructed to do in case of a disturbance. A moment before the officer walked into the room, the boys slid into their desks with uniforms straightened, backs stiff, and eyes forward, the likes of which I had not seen since the first day when I had been introduced to the class by an officer and one of the coordinators from the company that had hired me for the government contract.

When the thick-jowled officer sauntered into the room with a scowl on his face as if I had interrupted his nap, all the students stood up and snapped to attention next to their desks. He gazed at me as a representative of the infidel culture from which I came and shouted, "What is problem?"

"Two students were fighting, sir."

Turning to the students, he growled, "Who fighting?" He repeats the question in Arabic.

Silence.

He approached a cadet in the front row and stood nose to nose with him. "Who fighting?"

The student remained firm and loudly answered in rapid Arabic, probably so I wouldn't know what he said.

The officer turned his furrowed brow toward me. "He say he see no one fighting."

I stared at him. I was alone. My word against a room full of his countrymen, though he knew better than anyone the deceptions they were capable of. I could count on no one's support, not even the student I had sent to get the officer, the one who seemed most sympathetic, the one who had flirted with me on numerous occasions in a playful Saudi way.

That afternoon I had a meltdown on the tennis court, yelling, throwing my racket, and eventually storming off the court when my opponent called a ball out I knew was in. It was unlike me. I had become someone else, a demon version of myself and in danger of alienating one of the few friends I had on the base.

That same week, I had foolishly put my trust in Marvin, a gay colleague. I confided in him another colleague, Sam, had taken to following me around like a puppy dog and I feared he wanted me to help him come out. Sam was a sweet though nerdy guy, not at all my type. I barely kept things together myself and certainly didn't need the responsibility of someone else's happiness. Instead of offering advice, Marvin acted as if Sam's struggle was the funniest thing in the world. And the next time Sam asked if he could sit with us at lunch, Marvin said, nodding at me, "Should I leave? I'm sure you would like to be alone with your boyfriend. Too bad he doesn't feel the same way."

Sam's face reddened and he glanced at me with a look so hurtful I was afraid he might burst into tears. He took his tray and sat at a table alone.

"You're such an asshole, Marvin." I stood up and left the table to the cackle of his laughter.

The compound housed the instructors on the base, a gossipy small town where the inhabitants assuaged their boredom by being petty if not downright mean. The naval training staff, mostly retired U. S. military, hated the English teachers and called us faggots under their breath. They had no sympathy for our nearly impossible job of getting the students up to speed so they understood the naval training materials written in English. The students, in turn, were unruly, making a good portion of my job discipline. They hated the rigid military life and made my time there hell as much as they could get away with. On the next opportunity to leave the country I was seriously considering breaking contract. But for today, my goal was simply to escape the confines of the compound alone. I had gotten on a local bus and told no one where I was going.

My fellow travelers were lulled into various stages of drowsiness by the constant rocking of the bus, oblivious to what was happening, both inside the bus and outside the windows. I was a light-haired, blue-eyed American, the only Westerner in a sea of darker peoples—Yemenis, Pakastanis, Filipinos, Turks and Thais. They took no special notice of me since Americans and Europeans were quite common in this province of Saudi Arabia even though few of them braved public transportation. I enjoyed a sense of contentment all of us on the bus shared a similar plight, foreigners brought in to help build the modern Kingdom of Saudi Arabia, though admittedly with significantly different pay grades.

After passing truck farm after truck farm on the outskirts of town, we pulled into Qatif with its dusty, potholed streets and sand-colored buildings, the new structures not quite finished and the old ones allowed to crumble in place. Traffic slowed with the streets full of pickup trucks bringing wares to the market. Next to my window seat was a truck with a tarp thrown over a makeshift frame, and amongst the farmer's goods his three daughters lounged. In the relative privacy of the tarp-covered bed of the truck, the girls must have felt confident to peel back their black veils. They smile d and waved at me with surprising boldness. They were the first uncovered faces I had seen of Saudi women since I arrived in the country. I was frozen. If I even cracked a smile, I feared I could be arrested. The company literature made it abundantly clear you weren't supposed to as much as look at a Saudi woman, though in every town I had visited women were completely covered from head to toe in a black garment called an abaya. Not even their eyes were visible.

Since we had entered the town, I had already seen a number of women who wore a veil but with an opening for their eyes. Qatif was a Shiite stronghold, and attire differed from the Sunni Muslims dominant throughout the rest of the country. Despite the friendly reactions of the young ladies a few feet away, this minority sect of Islam had frequently displayed its less than warm feelings toward Westerners. I had been warned about coming here, particularly alone. My recently not so dear friend Marvin had told me that, during Khomeini-spurred riots in 1979, several Americans were roughed up. He told me he knew one of them and gave a complete account of what had happened. The National Guard, controlled by the dominant Sunni sect, swiftly stepped in and brutally squelched the uprising. I wondered what threads of bitterness still lingered in the air.

As I stepped off the bus, I was immediately caught in the somber gaze of three Arabs sitting on a bench who followed my every movement with suspicious eyes. I smiled and hurriedly escaped into a covered area with produce stalls, looking back several times to see if I was being followed. I tried to concentrate on the great piles of fresh fruits and vegetables giving off sweet and bitter smells. Mystery solved. Since our dining hall food showed a decided lack of fresh produce and the drabbest interpretation of American food cooked to oblivion by a British cook, my impression had been that fresh food was hard to come by in Saudi Arabia. Now I had proof my supposition was wrong.

I spied to my right a huge pile of melons, and in an instant a large one came into my field of vision in the hand of a wizened fruit seller holding a Bowie knife in the other. With a flick of the man's wrist, the blade carved into the tender orange flesh, stabbed the chunk, and it was under my nose with the shiny point of the knife protruding from the juicy morsel. I took it gingerly—I had little choice— and popped it in my mouth. The nectar ran down my chin. They were cheap, the man explained, making a low gesture with his hands, and I signed in return that they were too heavy to carry while I shopped. He wiped his knife on his thobe, a long shirt-like garment, and let the blade drop into a piece of wood. Then picking up two cantaloupes, he held them up to his chest like breasts, jiggled them, and laughed showing several missing teeth. I laughed in return, waved, and walked away carefully.

As I came to the end of the produce stalls, I was overpowered with the smell of fish, reminding me what know-it-all-but-often-correct Marvin had told me about Qatif being the largest fish market not only in Saudi Arabia, but the Persian Gulf. I looked down to see a pail of shimmering tiny fish, and next to it a bin of toe-thick prawns. Beyond that was a pail of blue crabs snapping at the air. I walked into an adjacent shed where the eyes of thousands of sea creatures pleaded for their lives, countless varieties of fish in all sizes and colors.

Two men walked by in fishgut-splattered aprons carrying a tub of bass and I was forced off the narrow boardwalk into a puddle of putrid water. The seafood, like the abundance of fresh produce, never made it to our dining hall. Nearly dizzy from the overwhelming odor of fish, I left the shed in search of the main market area.

Across the street from the food market, rugs and baskets were strewn out over a dusty street corner. Sellers liked to put new rugs from Pakistan and Afghanistan out in the street to be faded by the sun and trampled on, so they would look antique. In contrast, baskets were kept out of the sun under plastic tarps since the bright colors faded quickly.

The only rugs native to Saudi Arabia were Bedouin rugs with simple striped designs in browns, beiges and grays, some with threads of bright color running through them. The women selling them, all draped in black, were barefoot, but unlike their city sisters, their eyes were exposed, dark marbles on whites the color of stained teeth.

As soon as I focused on a rug that appealed to me, a woman held up her bangled arm and showed me four fingers, meaning four hundred riyals or over a hundred dollars. I scoffed and started to walk away, and in a split second she was down to three, chattering through her veil. I held up two fingers and she threw up her hands in outrage, her babble ramping up to a feverish pitch. Two I insisted, so she showed me a smaller, ugly rug perhaps made by a young daughter practicing her skills, and I moved to walk away again. She grabbed my arm.

I panicked. A Saudi woman was holding my arm, leaving me caught in a social, psychological, and physical trap all at the same time. She let go and held up three fingers again, but with a finger from the other hand cutting one of them in half. Now we were making progress, though we were still at about seventy bucks for a loosely woven rug, which in any other country in the Middle East would go for fifteen tops. The local women had the knack for milking the inflated economy of Saudi Arabia.

I took out two twenty-five and held it in her face. In a flash it was gone, disappearing into the folds of the woman's abaya as she walked away. I rolled up my rug and stuck it under my arm, doing a little dance of satisfaction my bargaining skills had improved considerably since I arrived in the country.

Down the street I wandered into the oppressive heat of the butchers' alley where huge carcasses hung on hooks, dripping blood onto the bare earth. Big cow eyes stared up at me from severed heads. There were lifeless tails too that did nothing to alleviate the fly problem, swarms forming big black spots on the sides of beef. From their exposed undersides hung enormous testicles attesting to the quality of meat, as one of the sellers who spoke English explained.

A bloody-aproned butcher caught me staring and waved me toward him with his large knife flashing in the sun. He wanted me to inspect the meat, pointing at the testicles with one and grabbing his crotch with the other. I pretended not to see him, once again taking up my search for the central market with my rug clutched tightly under my arm.

By following the crowds, I arrived at an extensive area of stalls alive with humanity, men in white and women in black. But the wares were a disappointing collection of what flea markets all over the world now sell—clothes, kitchen needs, drugstore products, and candy at prices slightly lower than discount stores.

But in one corner of the market was the area where birds and poultry were sold. This was a male domain where boys, six to sixty, fluttered about cages and boxes with air holes cut in them. Many of the birds and chickens and rabbits were being held aloft in uncomfortably looking ways by the buyers and sellers. Occasionally one would wriggle loose and take flight, causing a pack of boys to send up a shout and set out after the fleeing creature.

One man in a tight-clinging thobe with an uncovered head of black curls grabbed my hand and made me hold a pigeon. It was warm and I felt its heartbeat. I was sure the thing was going to shit in my hand, but even more afraid the smiley young man was going to try to give me the bird—a cherished gift one can't refuse in Saudi culture. His hands close to mine and the beating heart of the bird aroused me. The man stared into my eyes. After a couple minutes of observing the confusion in my face, he let up, took the bird back, and reached down to put it in a tiny box.

Next to the box with its perfect pair of warm small birds, a crippled old man sat in the dirt with pretzel-thin arms and twisted legs. A boy whisked by, dropping a one-riyal note in the skirt of his thobe. The man reached down to check its denomination—Saudi bills vary in size due to amount—staring into the distance with his cloudy eyes as his fingers danced around the edges of the bill.

I followed the man's gaze up toward the sky he couldn't see and let my dark mood drift away. Wallowing in my own problems had been replaced by immersing myself in scenes of ordinary people in an extraordinary place going about their business, rakish humanity keeping this precarious world spinning on its axis, the ancient exercise of buying and selling. I felt the importance of getting outside myself if only for a moment to experience the world around me. I realized how self-absorbed I had become. The royal blue sky and the bleached buildings made me think of a Greek island I had visited. For the first time in weeks I was happy to be in Saudi Arabia and I threw up my arms and shouted, "Alhamdulillah," a phrase I had learned not here, but in a Sufi dancing class back home some years before. Several people nearby gaped at me and smiled.

With a lighter step I headed for the sheep, goat, and camel market in a big parking lot. Since I had arrived in the country I had wanted to see a camel, but there were only two, and they were sitting side by side in the back of a pickup truck with their legs bound and tucked under them. To get closer to the camels I waded through a sea of brown sheep and multi-colored goats, which smelled of sour earth. And just as I reached out to touch the camel fur, a terrible bleating came from a goat that had been purchased and was being dragged away. I feared the protest might start a panic among the animals, but they all stood, roped together, looking dumb and apathetic.

As I weaved my way back through the animals, a fellow worker from the Navy base called out to me. It was Frank, the other long-term employee on the contract who, like Marvin, took young gay teachers under his wing. Marvin had come out to me first, and I had initially been impressed by his overseas experience, his endless tales of adventure. Seeing Frank reminded me of the frivolous tribulations and peculiar social dynamics back at the base, putting a check on my improving mood. But it was impossible to ignore him. He told me he was driving out to Tarout, an island off the coast and asked me if I wanted to go along. I had hoped to visit the island, and going in his car would make it a lot easier.

On the way across the causeway to the island, Frank

talked constantly, while at the same time smiling and waving at the drivers and passengers of other cars.

"Isn't this fun?" he said. "Maybe we'll see some of them on Tarout. There's a great cruising beach there." Everything I had heard about sex in Saudi Arabia made it sound risky, complicated, and unsatisfying. I had avoided going anywhere near the places Marvin had told me about, for which I was ridiculed and called a prude. And yet I was in the initial stages of excitement about the prospect of going to a cruising beach. It had been a dry first three months in the country.

We followed Riyadh Road, and later took a right at the sign for the little town of Darin, an enclave of mud and cinder block houses, which seemed to crumble even as I stared at them, though shiny new cars were commonly parked alongside and TV antennas sprung from the roofs.

On the outer shore was an old palace falling to pieces; only a few walls of mud brick construction remained and they were covered with graffiti. I wished I had learned to read the Arabic, knowing I couldn't truly understand the people until I was able to read the scribbles on the walls. Down by the water, teenage boys stripped down to their baggy undershorts, which became see-through when they went crab hunting in the water. They walked out into the low tide muck and picked up crabs with blue and orange shells. When they noticed us sitting on rocks watching them, they brought a couple of crabs over to show us. I reminded Frank to look at the crabs and how pretty they were all shiny wet as his focus had quite obviously moved to their dripping shorts.

Frank craned his neck to survey the area, and then took a camera out of his backpack. Photography was frowned on in most places in the Kingdom. He beckoned several of the boys to follow him. "I want to get some photos of the boys and their crabs with the palace ruins in the background. It would be a shoo-in for *National Geographic*. Or *Blueboy*," he said with a chuckle.

"I don't think it's a good idea, Frank." He gave me a pitying look, but I wanted no part of his schemes. "I'll stay here."

"Suit yourself."

I watched him with five or six boys in tow cross the road and head up to the ruins. Soon they disappeared behind a wall, and I returned to my rock facing the sea.

A short time later I heard shouting, but I imagined it came from several children down the way playing in the water. The tide was out and you could wade out quite far. Time passed and I began to worry. I saw one of the boys who had gone with Frank run down the beach to where the children were, grab a little girl by the hand, and hurry off in the opposite direction.

"Hey," I shouted to the boy. He didn't turn around.

Up near the ruins there was no activity. The other boys must have still been with Frank or had disappeared. The sun was low in the sky and the billowy clouds wore a skirt of color. It would be dark soon and we needed to return to the base. I made my way across the road and up toward the ruins. Like bats out of a cave, three boys ran out through one of the Arabic arches toward Riyadh Road, a look of fright on their faces.

"Hey," I shouted again, but they ignored me. "What have you done, Frank?" I said under my breath. Violent crime and murder were rare in Saudi Arabia, particularly directed at foreigners. Penalties were severe. But it didn't stop my mind from imagining the worst. I ran up the incline and through the arch the boys had just exited. A black cat sat atop a pile of rocks and stared at me.

Frank lay in the rubble, curled up in a ball with his broken glasses several feet away. "Frank!" As I got closer, I saw a couple of bloody wounds on his face, but he was breathing. "What happened?"

He moaned and spoke as if the words pained him. "I didn't do anything, I swear. I only wanted some pictures." His voice was full of phlegm, and tears streamed down his face. "The little bastards threw rocks at me."

"Can you stand up? We need to get you to the hospital and call the police."

"Oh, no, please. No hospital. No police. Help me up. Do you see my camera anywhere?"

"No. They must have taken it. Shit. What kind of pictures are on there?"

"I didn't touch them, I swear. We have to get out of here. Can you drive? My glasses are broken."

"Sure." His arm was around my shoulders, and as we walked to the car as swiftly as possible, we stumbled and nearly fell. "Careful," I said.

"I'll sort it out when we get back. Please, don't tell anyone about this. They could throw me out of the Kingdom."

"But if you didn't do anything…"

"Well, it's my word against theirs. You know how they are. Lying is nothing to them."

I should have been on his side, but I didn't believe him. We got to the car and I heard a siren in the distance. "What a mess!" I could be implicated in his dirty little game. If they didn't send me packing, I was definitely leaving next chance I got. It wasn't possible to hop on a plane. You needed an exit visa to leave the country and that had to be for a valid reason.

"Hurry," said Frank, as we slammed the car doors. "Don't take Riyadh Road. I'll direct you another way."

After skirting the island on a different road, we got on the main highway back to Dammam just as the prayer call revved up, the bellowing voice coming from various minarets in the area. I hadn't gotten used to the mournful invocation from the muezzin, markedly similar everywhere I had been, but in this moment it was a particularly stark reminder of where we were and what had just happened. My hands trembled and I grabbed the wheel tighter. Several of the cars pulled over.

"Do I have to stop?"

"No, it's not required. Just drive." Frank's voice seemed to echo the mournful quality of the caller. "I'm sorry about all this."

"God, Frank. What were you thinking?"

"Especially don't say a word to Marvin. He'd destroy me with a Cheshire grin and a bulge in his pants."

Back in my room, I kept looking out the window, expecting a police van to show up and whisk Frank away. My view became increasingly more hazy as the wind of the setting sun whipped the sand, turning everything to a pale beige. A car with its lights on inched along the road in front of the building, but it wasn't a police car. I closed the window to keep the grit outside.

I put on a windbreaker, hat and scarf over my face

and trudged to the dining hall. Sam sat alone at a table in the corner.

I placed my tray down across from him. "I'm sorry, I should have known you can't tell anybody anything in this place."

"I misjudged you."

The words stung. "What do you mean?"

"I hoped you were better than the others."

"I'm going to be better. I know that doesn't help you much, but I am. And then I'll probably leave."

Sam's eyes rose in horror. "Break contract?"

I scanned the room to see if anybody was within earshot. "The money is nice, but it isn't worth it. Please don't repeat what I said."

"I won't." He stood and picked up his tray. "Sorry. I've got to go."

He walked toward the tray window with hunched shoulders and a slow gait. For a brief moment, I imagined staying in the country and helping Sam go through whatever he was going through. I could be his friend and help him fend off the taunts from the others. The next moment a depressing realization gripped me, a gut-wrenching awareness I wasn't strong enough to do it.

# Manama Christmas

The old man stared at her accusingly from inside the third bedroom of their bungalow she had turned into a studio. Perhaps Sydney *had* been able to capture something in this painting, despite her general frustration, an ennui that at times made her want to slash a big red X on most of her work. She kept switching half-finished paintings on the easel to make it appear she was doing something. She wasn't. Hadn't completed a painting since they arrived in Saudi Arabia. She reached in, closed the door, and proceeded down the hall to the living room.

Her husband, Jim, had taken a teaching position at the King Faisal University in Dammam. They would stay long enough to save a down payment for a house back in Wisconsin. "You'll have lots of time to paint," Jim had said. "I'll be at work and Cammy will be in school." She had never been able to make him understand that artistic expression required more than time. It required inspiration, and in the case of painting, the right light. She needed to be surrounded by green trees and blue sky, and in winter by the pure whiteness of snow. Here the green on the compound's desperate attempt to bring life to the desert, the fake lawns and oleander bushes, were coated with a constant layer of dust, and the sky remained stuck in the yellow-brown spectrum.

As she reached the living room, the air conditioning grumbled to life in a not so subtle reminder of how everyone kept the outside outside, the heat at bay, living in a bubble not only against the weather, but also the culture she had no desire to adjust to, a culture that treated women as second class citizens more than any place she had been. The ache of being so far from family and friends was chronic and visceral. She shook her head at the pathetic tabletop Christmas tree cowering in the corner of the living room.

They had arrived in the country in October, and now it was almost the holidays. The tree had to be stuck in the corner where no one would see it from the outside. Outdoor Christmas decorations were strictly forbidden. It would be her first Christmas away from home, another fact that weighed on her, killed her spirit, and made her wander around the house as if she were an inmate at an asylum. The administration however, in its infinite tolerance of infidels, decided to give them a long weekend, and they had planned a trip to Bahrain where they might at least have a holiday cocktail. Alcohol was forbidden in the Kingdom.

She had shooed Jim and Cammy out of the house, saying she wanted to paint. It was the Moslem weekend, and Jim had organized an excursion to Hofuf, a city known for palaces and *souqs* or markets. Her husband and daughter seemed impervious to the heat, while Sydney melted under the sun, her pale skin turned beet red, and she felt every degree of radiant heat from buildings and walls as if they were needles. "You guys have a good time," she had said. "I'll make dinner."

She went back down the hall and threw open the studio door. "What do you want?" she shouted at the old man. His head was wrapped in a dirty cloth, and the wrinkles of his brown skin had been baked in, deep lines of hard living framing eyes that at times admonished her, and at others peered through her. She had to admit she'd done a good job on the eyes. Not so good on his long brown garment of rough wool that was soiled, tattered, and no doubt gave off a putrid smell of sweat. His hands, crossed in his lap as he sat hunched on a low wall, were swollen and discolored as if he had a vitamin-deficiency disease. She had worked from a hastily snapped photo as most Saudis balked at being photographed and occasionally became hysterical. It wasn't her preferred way of doing portraits, but in this case it was the only option. She took him down and made him face the wall. She mulled over which unfinished painting to replace him with when she heard the front door open. Time had flown by, and she had done nothing.

"We're home," said Jim.

"I'm in the studio. I'll be out in a minute."

She exited the studio and halfway down the hall, Cammy came to her, shouting, "Mommy!" and gave her a big hug.

"Did you have a good time, sweetheart?" She cranked up a smile and tried to sound cheerful. She steered her toward the living room.

"Yeah, and you know what? We went to an old fort and saw a man playing with his—"

"Cammy," her father said like a warning. "We can tell—"

"His thing!" Cammy blurted out with wide eyes. She went straight to the next story. "And this funny old lady ran after Daddy yelling and tried to grab his camera, and then..."

"Slow down, honey. Maybe Daddy ought to tell me."

"I already did," protested Cammy. "What's for dinner?"

"Looks like chicken," said Jim. A frozen chicken sat on the counter with a puddle under it.

"Is that okay?" She didn't have a clue how she was going to prepare it.

Jim walked over and tapped on the still frozen breastbone. "Hmm. Maybe we should go for Chinese."

"Yay!" said Cammy.

"We can have chicken tomorrow."

Jim glanced at his watch. "We'll have to hurry if we want to get in before prayer call." Restaurants were supposed to close during prayer times, but if they pulled down the shades and didn't let anyone go in or out until prayer was over, they could get away with serving their customers.

"Let me change," said Sydney. Her outfit, gym shorts and a tank top, was a clear no-no in public.

She put on a pair of culottes and a sleeveless blouse. The Saudis probably wouldn't like it, but she sure as hell wasn't going to cover herself up completely and sweat like a pig.

When she got to the front door, Jim frowned. "You're going to go like that?"

Sydney groaned and did an about-face.

"Wait, Syd." He grabbed a gauzy scarf from the coat rack. "You can wrap this around your shoulders. That should be good enough. We'll duck in and out of the restaurant."

In the car, Jim told his story of Hofuf. Cammy had fallen asleep in the back seat. "Cammy and I were looking at the old Turkish fort along with some young British women who had just gotten off one of those tour buses."

"I didn't think they had tourists in Saudi Arabia."

"I mean those shopping coaches they run every weekend from Aramco. Anyway, when we turned to go, I saw a young Arab boy about twenty feet away, standing astride his bicycle with his thobe pulled up to his waist. In clear view, his you-know-what was sticking out of his shorts and he was rubbing it while he watched the young British women."

"Did anybody do anything?"

"Most people didn't even seem to notice. A couple of the women tittered and glanced away."

"I think Westerners who stay here for any length of time stop seeing things. It's easier."

"It's like the opposite of culture shock. You become desensitized to the weirdness."

"I don't plan on becoming one of those zombies."

Jim sighed. "I know you hate it. Let's give it a year."

"I don't think I can spend another Christmas here." What she honestly wanted was to pack up her and Cammy's things and leave the next day. In a morning phone call, her mother had told her Wisconsin had its first big snowstorm. She could think of nothing better than making angels in the snow. But Jim would never have it. And it wouldn't be fair to leave him behind in this hell, even if he didn't seem to mind the conditions half as much as she did.

An uncomfortable silence fell on the car as they pulled into the parking lot. The owner of the restaurant was already beginning to lower the shades. "Hurry," said Jim.

Sydney woke up Cammy, and they got inside right before the Closed sign was turned around.

"What happened with the camera?" Syd asked once they had sat down in the family section of the restaurant. "You didn't lose your camera, did you?"

"Almost," said Cammy, rubbing her eyes.

"It was my own stupidity. As many times as I've been warned not to take pictures of Saudis, I couldn't resist. In the women's souq, a group of Bedouin women sat on the ground selling their wares—baskets and jewelry. Their black veils and primitive jewelry were such a contrast to the brightly colored umbrellas under which they sat. So I snapped a quick one from across the street. No one in particular, just a general picture. And bam! Like a shot out of a cannon, a woman came running across the street, veils and bangles to the wind, screaming at the top of her lungs. Cammy grabbed my hand and we were frozen there as she came barrelling down on us. In a split second she had her fingers wrapped around the strap of my camera and was trying to pull it out of my hand. I held on tight while she jabbered in Arabic. When I heard the word 'police' I realized the seriousness of it all. A crowd had gathered and the police would be there soon if I didn't do something. I whipped open the back of the camera and pulled out the film, dangling it in front of her. 'Here,' I said. 'Take it.' That shut her up, and she went away, holding the unraveling film at a distance like a poisonous snake. There were a hundred eyes on me, and Cammy had her head buried in my leg."

"I was scared, Daddy."

"I know, pumpkin. I'm sorry. I won't do that again."

When prayer time was over, they paid the bill and left the restaurant. "Can we get some ice cream?" said Cammy.

"Uh…" said Jim, looking at Sydney's bare shoulders.

"Sure," said Sydney. She wrapped the scarf around her. "I practically look like a nun."

The shopping center had a Baskin-Robbins, a Safeway, a Sizzler, and several other shops frequented by foreigners and wealthy Saudis. Now that prayer time was finished, many of the locals liked to drive their new shiny cars round and round the parking lot while foreigners strolled up and down the sidewalks. Darkness was falling, but the center was brightly lit by streetlights and the headlights of the cruising vehicles.

Each of them got their favorite flavor of ice cream and put all their attention to licking the treat before it melted down the cone and onto their fingers. Jim looked up and mumbled, "Oh, shit." Two thick-bodied Saudis in traditional dress—white thobes, and red and white *ghutrahs* on their heads—with canes in their hands and accompanied by a policeman in uniform were making a direct line toward them. The car was only twenty yards away. If they could…

Too late. Jim realized he was about to have his first encounter with the infamous *mutawa*, the religious police. One of the Saudis thrust a paper in Jim's face. It read: Woman Dress Code According to the Qu'ran.

"What is this?" said Jim, though he doubted pleading ignorance would be successful.

"Read" said the second man. The policemen stood at a distance.

"I don't believe this. This too much for one day," said Jim.

"What?" said the man. He twirled the cane in his hands. It was normally used to herd slackers into the mosques when prayer call was unleashed from the speakers.

"Never mind," said Jim. He studied the leaflet while ice cream melted over his fingers.

"Let me see *igama*," said the Saudi. Jim handed over his identity card. The man examined it and put it in his pocket. Jim had been told to never lose track of his *igama*.

"May I have my *igama* back?" The man pretended like he didn't understand.

Sydney stepped forward with Cammy clinging to her skirts. "Wait. He needs that card."

"Tell madam be quiet," said the Saudi. Officials never addressed women directly, always through their husbands or male relatives.

Sydney was flushed. "Do you have something to say to me?"

"Please, Syd," said Jim. "I'll handle this."

The second Saudi official smirked and shook his head. "Not good this."

A voice came from behind Sydney. "Excuse me. Maybe I can help. My English is so-so." She turned around and recognized Omar, the salesman from The European Clothes Shoppe they were standing right in front of. Her friend, Jennifer, her only friend in the Kingdom, had dragged her into the shop one day. "You've got to see this guy. He's Lebanese and drop-dead gorgeous. If they wouldn't kick me out of the country or give me forty lashes or whatever, I'd jump on him in a minute." Jennifer taught in the nursing school and her husband was back in the States. To say she was uninhibited was an understatement, and Sydney had heard about her escapades with some of the doctors. That day she had flirted with Omar while Sydney pretended to look at dresses.

Omar approached the Saudis and spoke to them in Arabic. In addition to his good looks, he was dressed in tight designer jeans and a polo shirt accentuating his physique. His manner with the Saudis was cool and confident. Both Sydney and Jim stared at him in amazement.

After a few minutes he turned to Jim. "Excuse me for saying this, but they believe your wife is improperly dressed, and her behavior is not...uh...ladylike. Sorry." He looked at Sydney and gave her a shy smile.

"No, I get it. It's just that I need my *igama*. We're going to Bahrain next week."

Omar spoke to the officials again and came back with a slip of paper. "This is your receipt. You must go to police station, pay the fine, and they return your card. What day you go to Bahrain?"

"On Thursday. The company has given us a few days for Christmas holidays."

"I think there is time. Where you stay? Sheraton?"

"Yes. How did you know?"

"Is nice place for foreign people. They have good bar," he whispered.

"Mommy, I want to go home," said Cammy. "My hands are sticky." She had dropped her ice cream cone when the commotion started, and Sydney had thrown hers in the trash bin.

"We'll go in a minute, sweetie."

"Your daughter is very beautiful," Omar said to Sydney. She had felt marginalized not only by their encounter with the Saudis, but her husband's chat with Omar. She realized, though, he had to be careful in public talking to another man's wife.

"Thank you so much for your help," said Jim. He stuck out his hand.

Omar took it, held it warmly, and then touched his heart. He bowed slightly to Sydney. "You all must come to my shop for tea one day. I can show you my business." He gave no indication he remembered meeting her before.

★

In the next few days, Jim got his papers back, they wrapped presents, and packed for their trip to Bahrain. Sydney had lunch with Jennifer and recounted their experience with the religious police. And though it felt completely out of place, Sydney played a Christmas CD in the house, not too loudly, over and over. The day came for their departure, and they packed up the car for the hour drive across the causeway from Al Khobar to Manama, Bahrain. They felt a giddy excitement as if going to the island paradise of Tahiti, and sang silly Christmas songs on the drive. A great weight lifted off Sydney's shoulders. She looked forward to going shopping at the Souq Bab Al Bahrain Jennifer had told her about where gold prices were great. She wanted to start a charm bracelet for Cammy and give it to her for Christmas.

The island was flat and dusty like Saudi Arabia, but the skyline in the distance revealed the modern, bustling city of Manama. Sydney smiled as she looked over and saw women driving cars, and though they wore headscarves, their faces were not covered. She couldn't wait to sit by the pool and drink a nice cold beer.

They had splurged on the hotel and were impressed by the elegant lobby of the Sheraton. "Look, Mommy!" Cammy screamed, pointing at the large Christmas tree over-decorated with lights, garland, and baubles, replete with piles of wrapped gifts at its base. It rose like a beacon of hope surrounded by polished brass railings, plush carpet, opulent chandeliers, and overstuffed chairs.

Jim spotted the bar, the Polynesian Room, and staggered toward it in the exaggerated cadence of a zombie. Sydney grabbed his arm. "Can we at least check in first?"

The suite was far more luxurious than any place they had ever stayed, a king-sized bed for them and a sleeping alcove with a screen for Cammy. A balcony overlooked the bay from the tenth floor. Sydney checked out the bathroom first thing and let out a shriek of delight at the huge soaking tub. "You done good, Mr. Haggerty," she said to her husband. He had already raided the mini bar and had a Heineken in his hand.

"Want one?"

"Oh, yeah!"

After a dinner in the hotel restaurant, Jim, who had been fidgety throughout the meal, announced he was going to the bar. "I'll help you put Cammy to bed first"

"I don't want to go to bed," said Cammy.

Sydney sighed. "You go ahead. I'll let her stay up a while, and then I'm going to take advantage of that tub."

"Okay, honey."

Sydney lay back in the warm water of the bath and tried to relax. If only she had said yes to the bath pillow when they were packing for Saudi Arabia, instead of discarding it in an attempt to show practicality. Meeting a balance between need and want had never been her forte; whichever way she leaned, she inevitably had regrets about it later. But by reaching for a hand towel and folding it in quarters, she created a suitable if somewhat lacking substitute for the air pillow. Now, with her head cushioned against the hard surface of the tub, she closed her eyes and let her mind drift.

She was transported back to the bungalow on the compound, and through the window came the spin-chirp of the water sprinkler, a constant reminder of the dryness of the land, and the bounce-thomp from the tennis courts, a less regular reminder some attempts had been made to make their life more bearable. Occasionally the two sounds fell into sync, creating a sort of oom-pa-pa rhythm, chirp-bounce-thomp, chirp-bounce-thomp.

The rhythm was suddenly broken by a noise from inside the house. Was it the air conditioner? Or her husband's car pulling into the carport? But it was neither. This was a steady thump, steps moving through the house until it stopped outside the bathroom door. Her body remained motionless like a log in a still pond, but her heart pounded rapidly, and her mind raced through a myriad of possibilities.

The door opened slowly, revealing a tall dark figure standing in the near-darkness of the hallway. A scream began in her throat, but could not be pushed from her lips. An impulse to modesty made her want to cover her body, but she was paralyzed. He stepped into the room, focusing his emotionless brown eyes on her nakedness, and moving his thick pouty lips under a heavy moustache, he said something. Though she couldn't hear what it was, she recognized Omar, the Lebanese clerk from the European Clothing Shoppe. Her mind skipped over the details of how he got there, accepting it was the inevitability of destiny which brought them together. Desire had a way of cutting through a thousand years of cultural and religious taboos. All fear was gone; instead, she worried about how horrible she must look without any makeup and her hair a mess. In spite of her appearance, his rugged good looks were riveted on her fair features, and she could already taste the exotic sweetness of his lips.

With Sydney locked in the grasp of his ancient eyes, he unbuttoned the rest of his half open silk designer shirt. Inside was a gold medallion in the shape of a book resting in the thick hair of his wide chest. Letting the shirt fall to the floor, he reached down into the water. She watched the hair of his arm gradually become plastered to his shiny dark skin as his gentle hand found her breast. Then far,

far away, a phone began to ring. The jingle came closer and closer until she could no longer ignore it was the hotel phone.

"Damn!" she screamed as she opened her eyes to the soft light of the master bathroom, a far cry from their bathroom back on the compound. She had called her mother earlier and left a message for her to call back. She jumped out of the water. Still dripping wet, she threw on the hotel caftan and ran to the phone. As she picked it up, the line went dead.

"Of course ," she yelled, slamming down the receiver. She peered at the wet spot on the hotel rug and wanted to cry. Walking back down the hall, she switched on lights, noticing Jim was not back. She checked on Cammy, who was sound asleep, and turned on the TV, which offered a full array of international channels. She dozed off and woke up after midnight. Jim had still not returned. She dressed hurriedly, checked on Cammy again, and slipped out of the room.

Jim sat at the bar talking with another man. It all appeared rather normal, and she felt guilty about standing inside the doorway in the shadows, spying on her husband. A moment later, the man he was talking to turned his head. It was Omar. She was at first excited and wanted to rush in and say hello. But wait, how had he happened to show up in Bahrain on the same weekend, at the same hotel? Ah yes, the conversation outside his shop on the night of the *mutawa*. But...

She held back, biting her lower lip, watching them laugh at each other's jokes, lean close like lovers, Omar frequently touching Jim's arm. The attractive cocktail waitresses in floral print dresses with flowers in their hair in the theme of the bar moved about without so much as a glance from the two men.

A chill ran down her spine. How could she have been so stupid? She wasn't in denial. She swore there had been no signs, unless it was a decided decline of interest in sex over the last couple of years, which she had chalked up to the seven-year crisis point so many marriages went through. In the next moment, she felt ridiculous. She remembered parties in college, in the new age of male bonding and touching, when drunk guys would paw each other and sometimes pass out in a drunk cuddle. Few if any of them turned out to be gay. She hadn't actually witnessed any damning behavior on the part of her husband except him indulging his tendency to drink to excess.

Jim asked for the bill. Omar tried to grab the check, and they playfully fought over it, batting each other's hands, leaning on each other until Jim won out. They stood up, unstable, Jim fell back on the stool. Omar took his arm and lifted him up, threw his arm around Jim's shoulders as they walked out of the bar. In the Arab world, affection between males was common. It wouldn't draw suspicion. Sydney moved behind a partition and watched them stagger toward the elevators. Jim whispered something to Omar, and Omar answered, perhaps too loudly, "Four. It's my lucky number." And they laughed.

Sydney ran up the stairs to the fourth floor. She opened the door as quietly as she could and coaxed it softly back into place. She tiptoed down the corridor and peeked around the corner at the two men making their way down the hall arm in arm. She didn't have to worry about them spotting her as they were wrapped up in each other, eyes dancing, body language anticipating what was coming next. They stopped at a door. Omar pushed Jim against the wall and planted his lips on his. Jim responded in kind. When was the last time Jim had kissed her with so much fervor? Jim paused and pushed him away, but not too hard. "Not here," he said. Omar pulled the key out of his pocket, slipped it in the slot, and pulled Jim into the room.

Not long before they left for Saudi Arabia, Sydney and Cammy had gone to a playground to use Cammy's favorite slide, a high and fast one. She encouraged her mom to try it. Sydney went down the slide, her feet out in front of her, and gaining speed, she hit the ground on her butt with unexpected force. It shocked her and knocked the wind out. That was exactly the feeling she had at that moment, stunned, confused, and unable to breathe. She slid to the floor and considered her options. She could go pound on the door and demand her husband back or return to the room and act as if she had seen nothing. She went through the door to the stairs, walked up to the next floor, and caught the elevator to the tenth.

She lay in bed, staring at the ceiling, going through every possible time Jim could have been out pursuing his desires. She hated him for making her feel so clueless. Why had she seen no red flags? Last month he and a group of coordinators in his department had gone to Bahrain for a "retreat" weekend. Back in Wisconsin, he would occasionally go out with his old college buddies, or so he said, and not come back until the morning. Several times he went to teachers' conferences in cities like Chicago, New York, and San Francisco, telling her it would be boring for her to accompany him. Since he didn't flirt with other women, she never suspected he was having an affair when their sex life waned. He had always been a loving husband and an adoring father. This couldn't be happening to her.

She feigned sleep when he crawled into bed at exactly 2:13 in the morning. The bastard kissed her on the top of her head.

In the morning, she and Cammy went down to an extravagant breakfast buffet with delicacies both Western and Middle Eastern while Jim slept in. Her daughter patted her arm. "Are you okay, Mommy? You look so serious."

"I'm fine. I didn't sleep well. Strange bed, you know." She scanned the dining room for signs of Omar. What if she ran into him? What would she say? She smiled at her daughter. "Do you want another waffle, sweetie?"

"No, thanks. I want to go to the pool. I want Daddy to come with us so I can stand on his shoulders and he can whoosh out of the water and I jump off. That's our favorite game."

"I'm sure he'll come to the pool later." She had to remain calm for Cammy's sake, but in her head, she was planning their exit, hers and Cammy's. Maybe they could be home before New Years. Holiday decorations would still be up.

Cammy was in the kiddie pool and Sydney was stretched out on a lounge chair nearby. She was half asleep when Cammy yelled, "Daddy!" Jim waved at his daughter and came over to Syd's chair. He bent down to kiss her, and she turned away. "I'm all sweaty," she said.

"Did you eat?" He wore sunglasses, a tank top, and flowery board shorts she had never seen before. He plopped on the chair next to her.

"The buffet was incredible. Cammy ate two whole waffles." She attempted to keep her voice normal, only speak of everyday things.

"Daddy, I want to go in the big pool."

"In a minute, honey." And to Sydney, "God, I need a Bloody Mary."

"Hmm," she said, without interest, without any intention of asking about last night, what time he returned to their room, who he talked to in the bar.

"You'll never believe who I ran into. Remember the guy from the shopping center?"

Anger made a prickly course through her veins. So this was how he was going to play it. "The hairy one?"

Jim moved his sunglasses down his nose and stared at her. "Yes, the hairy one."

"Daddy, come on."

Jim took a deep breath, let his sunglasses fall to his lap, and rubbed his eyes. "I guess I better go." He stood and went over to Cammy. He picked her up and they went in the big pool. A few minutes later Omar appeared on the other side of the pool, took off his shirt, and sat at a table under an umbrella. His body was even more spectacular, more muscular than she had imagined, and yes, hairy. She couldn't stop the images from traipsing through her brain of Jim and Omar rolling around on the bed, the drunken passion, the sounds Jim made when he was about to orgasm. What could have driven her husband, not simply to men, but that type of man? She lowered her sunglasses and stared straight across at Omar.

He stood up as if the the power of her gaze had lifted him. Jim glanced at Omar and froze. The world ground to a halt, and even the birds that had been so noisy a few moments before went silent. One second. Two seconds. Three seconds. Four. "Daddy, let's do it again."

Omar walked around the pool to Sydney. "Good morning, madam. This is quite a surprise."

"Surprise?" Sydney let out a garbled laugh and pushed her sunglasses back up on her nose, not giving him the courtesy of seeing her eyes.

"Perhaps you don't remember me. I—"

"I know exactly who you are." Her voice had the grit of sandpaper.

"I'm sorry. Have I offended you?"

Sydney let out another disgusted chuckle. "I don't think offended is the right word."

Jim had tried to ignore their conversation, but now he stared at them, fear lining his face.

"Excuse me for bothering you. I will go."

"Not so fast. I wanted to ask you if you had a good time last night."

"This is a mistake."

"What? Talking to me or...?"

Jim was now out of the water and hurrying toward them.

Sydney's attention was drawn to the pool. She jumped up and pointed at her daughter "Cammy!" she said in a scream that reversed the flow of blood in her body. Jim had left her in the pool, and she had ventured toward the deep end where she could no longer touch the bottom. Her little arms flailed. "You idiot!" She ran toward the pool. Omar beat her to it, dove in, grabbed

Cammy and brought her to the edge. Jim and Sydney lifted her up. She coughed and sputtered. Sydney embraced her daughter, pulling her away from the two men.

Jim reached out to comfort his daughter. "Don't you dare!" Sydney snarled at him.

Cammy began to cry. "You're okay, sweetie. Just breathe." She patted her lightly on the back. "Everything's fine." She led her to the chairs and wrapped her in a towel. "Lie down here with me. You're okay." She continued to cough and sniffle. After a few minutes, she and Cammy went to the room.

★

When Jim came back to the room, Cammy was down for a nap. "Syd, what the hell is going on?"

Sydney stood at the window gazing out over the desert and beyond. "I think that's the question I should be asking, should have been asking these last few years."

"I can explain."

"What part would you like to explain? Kissing a man in the hallway of a hotel in an Islamic country?"

"Oh, fuck! You followed me?"

"You actually believed it wouldn't come out, that you could go on hiding indefinitely? I don't know which one of us is a bigger fool."

"I tried to talk to you, but I couldn't, couldn't risk losing Cammy." He glanced at Cammy's alcove. "This is not the time. Let's try to get through Christmas. We'll sort things out when we get to Saudi."

"Sort things out? I can't even respond to that. Look, here's what's going to happen. Cammy and I are taking the car and going back to the compound this very afternoon. You can continue your little fling or whatever it is."

Jim fell into a chair. "You can't."

"Don't tell me what I can and cannot do."

"You can't drive in Saudi Arabia. Remember?"

"Shit!"

Jim spoke softly. "I can't tell you how sorry I am. I had no intention of hurting you and Cammy. We need to go through with our Christmas plans for Cammy, open our gifts and all that. At least here we can celebrate Christmas. By the way, Omar is going back to Al Khobar this afternoon. I won't see him anymore."

"You're pathetic. This is way beyond, 'Sorry, honey, I got drunk and had a one-night stand with a woman I met in a bar.' I could compete with a bar floozy. But a hairy, muscular Middle Eastern man is a bit out of my range."

"He jumped into the pool to save Cammy."

She laughed at how quickly he had jumped to defend Omar. "I must remember to thank him. And maybe I should throw in a Merry Fucking Christmas!"

"Uh...he's a Moslem."

"Mommy, that's a bad word." Cammy stood behind them, rubbing her eyes.

"You're right, sweetheart. I'm sorry."

"Can we open our presents now? I can't wait for you to see what Daddy and I got you in Hofuf."

Jim and Sydney stared at each other. The good

memories crept into her head, but she cut them off. She wasn't ready for that phase to begin. She let out a toxic puff of air long stuck in her lungs. "I think that's a good idea."

# Miguel Mio

The knock at the back door caused me to spill the overly full cup of tea I was carrying from the counter to the table. Visitors were rare, and more so in the middle of a rainstorm. I lived alone on a plot of land carved out of the Mexican jungle, miles from the nearest town. The only other people normally on the property were the workers, and they had been sent home when the rain became heavy in the early afternoon.

I opened the door and felt the cool dampness infused with the fragrance of tropical green. The sight of the young man at the door made me take a step back. He looked like a deranged scarecrow that had been left out in the rain. His head was unprotected from the shower pouring off the roof as he gripped his straw hat in his hands. His black hair was plastered to his skull, and his white shirt with pearl snaps clung to his bony frame, transparent to the skin, revealing a tuft of dark chest hair.

He raised his eyes and I had to stop myself, as I always did in such moments, from being propelled into a fantasized future of extreme bliss. They were soft, brown and earnest, with lashes of exaggerated length. How many times had I let myself be led down an empty road by that look? My hand trembled on the handle of the door.

"Miguel Santos Ramirez, at your service, *señor*. I have come to humbly request you find it in your goodness to give me work." His absurdly formal Spanish had the curious effect of relaxing me, almost to the point of laughter.

And then a small voice escaped from behind the waterfall. "Me, too." I had been so taken with the young man's eyes I hadn't noticed he wasn't alone. A boy's head, more big black eyes than anything, appeared from behind the man's right hip, water rolling from his small round chin.

Miguel cuffed the boy on top of his head. "With respect, Vitico. Address the man as *señor*. Sorry, *señor*. I present my little brother Victor. We call him Vitico."

Rain continued off the roof and fell in a steady stream on Miguel's head and then down over his high cheekbones. He remained steadfast, unflinching.

"Please, come out of the rain," I said.

The boy started to rush forward, but Miguel clamped his hand on Vitico's neck and held him. He bowed his head and focused his gaze on his shoes. His jeans were relatively new but a couple of sizes too short, giving a clear view of the black, rounded-toe tie shoes of the kind the locals normally saved for Sunday mass, now soggy and caked with mud. "We couldn't, *señor*," he muttered.

"I insist. Look." I pointed at the floor. "It's already dirty. This time of year I don't worry about it." I ushered them into the kitchen, but they stayed close to the wall, dripping onto the mat where my muddy boots had been hurriedly discarded, one toppled over on the other. Miguel peered at my boots as if he was bothered by the disorder. I picked up the vagrant boot and set it upright. It was so quiet I heard droplets of water from their clothes hitting the rubber mat.

"Let me get you some towels."

"Oh, no, please. Don't trouble yourself, *señor*."

"No trouble at all."

When I came back with towels, Miguel had a firm grip on the back of Vitico's collar. I imagined Miguel to be in his late teens and Vitico about seven. The boy's eyes drank in all the details of the room. And there was a lot to look at in my house of curiosities. While my new home was being built, I had moved into the "hacienda," as the real estate agent had described it, though it was more of a large cabin. I neither liked the location nor the style of what had been a summer retreat for one of the few wealthy families in Acalán. When I first visited the land, I got the idea to build a grand house near the waterfall, knowing it would be a major project here in the jungle.

The distribution of rooms in the cabin was wrong, but the large open kitchen and dining area had become a repository for everything from construction materials to my unpacked boxes. Against the rustic walls my shiny stainless European kitchen gadgets—microwave, toaster oven, espresso machine, juicer, and blender—looked terribly out of place. Braids of garlic and onions hung from the walls next to framed art posters, and a large basket of fruit sat on the table. Crystals dangled in the windows to catch the sunlight and throw rainbows on the walls and the cabinets full of Italian glassware. The sink was overflowing with dirty dishes, colorful ceramic cups and plates I had collected in Spain. On the floor I had Turkish carpets, and several of my oddly shaped metal sculptures were hanging from the ceiling or propped against walls. In the corner were two canaries in a pagoda-shaped birdcage. I was sure the brothers had never been in a house quite like mine.

Miguel took one of the towels and rubbed the boy's head, and then dropped it over his shoulders. Vitico grabbed a corner and wiped his face. His eyes had gone from surveying the room to now watching my every move, suspicious of what kind of person could live in such exotic clutter. Miguel, on the other hand, only seemed concerned with trying to minimize their intrusion. He kept looking at the floor where they had dripped and tracked in mud, all the time having a watchful eye on Vitico lest he dart away and cause a disturbance.

"Would you like to see the birds?" I said to Vitico.

He nodded. I took his arm, gently pulling him away from Miguel, and led him to the cage.

"Don't touch anything," said Miguel.

Vitico gazed at me with a tiny roll of his eyes. I winked at him.

When we got to the cage, Vitico asked, "Why don't they sing?"

"They usually sing in the morning, and they're shy when there are new people around."

I glanced back at Miguel. He had dried his own head and his shiny dark curls had sprung to life. He caught me looking at him and his eyes returned to the mess on the floor.

Vitico stared at the birds like a hungry cat, and the canaries flitted about the cage.

"How did you get here?" I asked Miguel from across the room.

"We got a ride in the back of a truck up to Alvarado Road and walked from there." I shook my head. It was a two-mile walk from Alvarado Road on a steep gravel drive dangerous in the rain.

"Most days I only need five men and I have my regulars. Occasionally I have a big project where I need more. The work is hard."

Miguel didn't look particularly strong. We were building roads, clearing jungle, and laying the foundation for the new house. Things moved slowly during the rainy season. I had gone down that morning to pick up the crew in my truck. A local man named Juan had emerged as a leader and took charge of getting the workers, mostly his relatives. They were short, stocky and round-faced. He was proud of his position and made it clear that next to me, *el patrón,* he was in charge. He wouldn't think much of Miguel. Aside from being skinny, he clearly wasn't one of Juan's relatives.

"I can work hard, *señor.*"

"I'm sure you can. It's just that—"

"Please, *señor,*" Vitico blurted out. "He's really strong. I want to work, too. Our father is sick and—"

"Vitico," Miguel warned. He motioned for Vitico to come back by his side. He gathered the soggy towels and held them out to me. "Sorry to bother you, *señor.* We will go now."

"Wait. I didn't say no. There's plenty of work. The problem is the weather and getting supplies. I order materials and they don't arrive. I sometimes have to send the men home because there is nothing to do." I turned to Vitico. "Young man, I think you'll have to wait a few years. But what do you say I give your big strong brother a chance?"

Vitico cast his eyes down and twisted his mouth into a grimace. Miguel prompted him with a slight jerk to the back of his collar. "Yes, *señor.*"

"I pick up the workers in the central square at 6:30 in the morning. If you're late, it's a long walk." It was difficult for me to exhibit the stern manner of a boss, even though I had learned the workers expected it. But it was particularly difficult with this young man, who had managed to capture my curiosity in a short time.

"You make me very happy," said Miguel. He stuck out his hand, still cold and wet, but the grip was surprisingly strong. A tingling charge of anticipation went straight to my heart and flooded me with an overwhelming need to take care of him. Long after they left I was warmed by the memory and chilled by the prospect.

Miguel always arrived at the pick-up stop on time if not early. He worked hard and learned rapidly. I had to strive to not show him preferential treatment, and to pull my eyes away when I caught myself gazing at him with an increased tempo in my heart. My foreman, Juan, didn't say anything, but I could tell he wasn't pleased I had hired someone outside of his cadre of relatives and *compadres*.

I had a vague vision of what I wanted to create in my jungle paradise. It was loosely based on Gaudi's Parque

Güell in Barcelona, a wilder version due to the terrain, but incorporating *trencadís* or broken tile mosaics. Juan was good with the workers, but he didn't understand my vision. In a few short conversations with Miguel, I felt he could share my dream for what I would call Parque Escondido.

After a few weeks, I stopped caring what Juan and the other workers thought if I showed special interest in Miguel. I was the boss, paying their salaries to feed their families. At the end of the workday, I sometimes told Juan to take one of the trucks and drop off the workers. Miguel would stay with me and we would sit on the concrete of what would be the front porch of my house, facing the waterfall. In a nearby bush we heard a songbird Miguel called a *primavera*. The golden late afternoon sun cast long shadows, and the *primaveras* tweeted and warbled in an endless loop of joy, nearly drowning out the patter of falling water in the distance. Contentment fell like a blanket over me. I hadn't experienced such innocence and peace for a long time.

One afternoon I brought out a book on Gaudi. I told him about my time in Barcelona, exploring the wonders of the city's most famous architect. He was hungry for details about the outside world and mesmerized by the pictures I showed him, photos of the Sagrada Familia, Parque Güell, Casa Batlló, and other works. His expression told me my dream made sense to him.

Miguel turned to me, his dark eyes infused with golden light. "Let's go for a walk. I want to look at what we have done so far, to see it with fresh eyes." I loved the fact he used we, *nosotros*. In a moment, he had become an integral part of the plan

We walked along the trails and each plant and tree oozed a new, enhanced moisture, giving the impression we were walking through a magical greenhouse. Long chains of sleepy red and yellow acanthus blossoms hung alongside ivy ready to retake the trail. And later we came upon a clearing, a respite from the dense jungle where a prototype of the benches I envisioned throughout the property sat in a spot of late afternoon light. Not a single straight angle existed in the curvy cement bench, embedded with pieces of broken tiles in a mosaic pattern, but unlike the undulating benches in Barcelona's Parque Güell, this one was only six feet long, and the tiles were not Spanish, but Mexican from local factories. The workers gazed at me with wide eyes when I showed them a picture of what I wanted, and they observed in horror as I smashed Talavera tiles into small pieces.

"Yes! I see now," said Miguel with the excitement of a child. "We can have these benches everywhere, many places, like near the waterfall, in the garden of the new house. It will be so beautiful."

He understood the organic shapes of Gaudi and the sculptures I hoped to build, coming up with the word *organico* on his own in his language. I was overjoyed he understood my vision and desperately wanted to wrap my arms around him, never let him go. But I couldn't do it. His mother, Dona Miriam, had invited me to her home several times for meals. It pained her to know a single man had to eat alone in a house in the middle of the jungle. I sat around the table with Miguel, Vitico, Dona Miriam, and Don Pepe in their humble home filled with warmth and the smell of fresh-made tortillas. They trusted me completely, and to impose myself physically on Miguel would be an abuse of that trust. At the same time, they never asked me why I wasn't married or if I had a girlfriend. As an only child who lost my parents when I was a teenager, making me a man of inherited wealth, I loved sitting at their humble table, feeling an abundance of a different kind, something that couldn't be bought.

On the way back to the house, we took the path leading to the creek. A flock of parrots screeched in the trees above us as we moved along the trail to a bridge over a creek with a waterfall feeding into it. In the middle of the creek, right below the falls was a large rock. We stopped on the bridge and beneath us the water gurgled over the shiny stones as we leaned on the rail, breathing in the dense tropical air. I had the sensation the bridge was moving, that we were floating down the stream in a boat, Miguel and I drifting into the future.

"I have an idea," he said. "We can construct a broken-tile creature on that rock like you showed me in the book, except instead of a dragon, it would be a Mexican iguana. When the sun hits it like it is right now, it will shine. Maybe we use some little pieces of glass."

"I love that. I'm so happy you're taking an interest." My joy was interrupted by the dentist-drill buzz of mosquitoes around my ear, and I started swatting.

"We'd better go. These mosquitoes love *gringos*," he said with a laugh. He had taken to acting and speaking less formally, even making jokes I would have imagined impossible the first day I met him.

Next we came to the clearing where the foundation for the new house had been staked out. I removed a notebook from my pocket where I made drawings of ideas I had. I showed him some sketches of the house, which I had copied from Gaudi houses in Spain.

"But we are not in Spain. This is Mexico. You must make it more Mexican." He spoke passionately, and then realizing he might have overstepped, he added, "Sorry. It is your house. You must do what you want."

"No. You are absolutely right. Tell me how we can improve on the design." We discussed how to make it a hacienda, the living quarters gathered around a central courtyard with a fountain in the middle and the back end facing the waterfall. As I watched him speak excitedly, I couldn't stop myself from imagining we would one day live there together.

★

The heat was heavy with the moisture of late summer, making it a grueling workday. I worked alongside the men, putting in the hours and relishing the sense of accomplishment at the end of the day. And someday when the house and gardens by some miracle were all done, I would be able to look at my calloused hands with a feeling of pride.

When the other men piled in the truck to leave, I said in a low voice to Miguel, "We could go for a swim if you'd like to stay."

Juan hung out the window of the driver's side. "Hey, Miguel. You coming?"

I told him I would drive Miguel down later. The architect had recently dropped off new sketches and floor plans based on our changes, and we were going to look them over.

"*Claro, jefe,*" said Juan, but his expression barely contained a smirk questioning why I hadn't shown them to him first.

After they left, Miguel had a look of concern on his face. I asked him if Juan and the other workers treated him well. He shrugged.

"What do you mean?"

"They make some jokes. They call me *profe* (professor) since I finished high school and none of them have. No big deal."

I had caught bits and pieces of their riding him and it went beyond calling him professor. They were discreet when I was nearby, but I was sure they were less so when I wasn't.

We were sweaty and dirty. I tried not to stare at the damp spots on Miguel's work shirt where he had sweated through. "Let's go swimming first, and we can look at the drawings later."

He focused on the ground. "Uh, I have no..."

"You can borrow a pair of trunks." There was no reason we couldn't swim nude since no one was around, but I needed to maintain a semblance of propriety.

We followed a trail into the woods, which intersected with a path that led down to the bridge crossing the creek, and followed another path to the swimming hole below the waterfall. The waterfall was a fraction of what it had been in the spring, but still provided a calming murmur as it slid over the moss-covered rocks and rained down on the pool.

I indicated some bushes where he could change into the trunks.

"Ay, such modesty. We are men, no?" He stripped off

his dirty work clothes and baggy briefs, and slipped into the trunks before I had a chance to formulate an answer. Flashes of his nude body would carry me through long, dark nights. He waded in and dove under, coming up near the waterfall.

"*Hijole*," he shouted.

"Is it cold?"

"Refreshing. The water is not deep and it gets a lot of sun, so it's not too bad. Come on, *viejo.*" I hoped he was using "old man" as a term of endearment rather than referring to my age. I guessed I was about ten years older, though I still didn't know his exact age.

I changed into my trunks and dove in the water, coming up close to him. He moved directly under the waterfall, and waved for me to join him. "It's not cold at all," he said with a laugh.

"Liar."

I moved close to him and we let the chilly water rain down on our heads, causing me to shiver. I had to admit, though, it was something like paradise, pictures I had seen as a kid in *National Geographic* where I fantasized being with a loved one. The hollow drumming on our skulls made the waterfall somewhat less romantic than the pictures, but my remembrances of the day would warm the image significantly.

I backed out of the waterfall and turned to look at him standing waist-deep in the pool. Since he had come into my life, I hadn't seen him with his shirt off, and I was surprised he was in good shape, not muscular but toned. He was a man, and yet still a boy, vulnerable and wide-eyed. His attention appeared to drift into a distant memory.

I splashed him. "Hey, Miguel. Where are you?"

Miguel, at first stunned, splashed back, setting off a round of juvenile splashing. After a time our skin showed goose bumps, and we climbed out of the water onto the flat rock where we discussed putting a tile-encrusted iguana. We stretched out like seals basking in the warmth of the sun while the birds of the jungle called to one another over our heads. Our arms were inches apart. My heart pounded in my chest, which I told myself was from the exertion in the water. I balled my fists to stop myself from throwing my body on top of his. He covered my fist with his hand. "Relax, George." It was the first time he had called me by name instead of *jefe*. I unclenched my fist, and instead of taking back his hand he let it rest there, slowly lacing his fingers with mine.

"Are we doing something wrong?" Miguel asked.

"No," I croaked.

"Then why are you so nervous?"

"I think you know why."

"We are in our own world here. Let all your troubles go. Everybody is far away. Only the birds and maybe a few small animals nearby. I feel peaceful and happy."

I followed his advice and stopped worrying. We lay back, eyes closed, holding hands, until the sun no longer made rays of light on the back of our eyelids.

I opened my eyes and saw a pair of electric blue butterflies chase each other above us in a shaft of golden light. They dipped and dived, darted away, and then came back. Their wings shimmered with an otherworldly intensity. One landed on Miguel's head and perched on a thick strand of wet hair. It fluttered its wings slowly and became still.

"Don't move. Stay right there. Don't move. Don't move," I whispered. I wanted to look upon this beautiful sight forever, his slightly parted lips, his serene face, the eyelashes, the butterfly settled in his thick dark hair.

He opened his eyes and the butterfly took flight. "What is it?"

"Look." Above us now were hundreds of blue butterflies. They danced in the air for several minutes, and in an instant were gone.

"It's like a dream," he said.

"It will be dark soon. We should go back."

We gathered up our clothes, only putting on our shoes for the walk back.

Miguel had not been in my house since the day he and Vitico arrived in the pouring rain to ask for work. In front of me in the low light of the kitchen was a completely different person from a few months before. A bottle of Herradura on the table caught his eye. "Very good tequila," he said.

"Would you like some?"

He titled his head slightly and raised his eyebrows. "Well..."

The first shots we downed hurriedly as if we had someplace to go. I heated up food and handmade tortillas Doña Miriam had sent with Miguel. We kept drinking. We examined the new architectural drawings, bouncing ideas off each other. The time flew by.

"It's late," I said. "I should take you home."

"No way. You cannot drive."

"Your mother will worry."

"Mothers always worry. It's not the first time I don't sleep at home."

"You're staying here?" My voice was heavy with a gift from the gods arriving too suddenly. "You can have the bed. The sofa is fine with me."

He shook his head like a teacher feeling pity for a slow student. He scooted his chair back from the table, bridged the short distance between us, leaned down, and kissed me on the lips. "The bed is big enough, no?"

His lips tasted of the mystery of aged tequila, sweet and peppery. I had known this young man to be sweet, but I was unfamiliar with the peppery side, never could have imagined it. But even in my loosened inhibitions, images galloped through my head of Juan and his men barging through the door and catching us, or worse, Vitico looking for his brother. I broke off the kiss.

He gave me a pat on the cheek and lifted me to my feet, enveloping me in his arms. He whispered, "Don't worry about my mama. I'm a big boy and can do what I want."

I locked the door and we stumbled into the bedroom still wearing our now dry swimming trunks. We fell onto the bed, too drunk to do anything but cuddle, a tangle of arms and legs with the ceiling fan spinning backward and forward above us and the darkness outside cloaking us in its cocoon.

In the morning I was the one with doubts, the one who wasn't able to smile. We were from different worlds, but we were both part of a community. I didn't believe isolation and darkness could hide us. He was an employee, who had to interact with my other employees every day. At least it was a Sunday, and we didn't have to face the others. My heart longed to build something while my over-thinking brain worked to tear it down.

He shuffled into the kitchen. "I smell coffee." He didn't approach me with a kiss as a lover might, but approached the birdcage and said, "*Buenos dias, chiquitos,*" as if it was something he did every day.

"I'll fix breakfast and then drive you home."

"You don't have to worry, you know. Everybody in town knows I have a girlfriend. She wants to get married, but I don't want it. I don't even like her that much."

I assumed he was trying to reassure me, implying that I might have hope, but his words did the opposite. It struck me at that moment I had to do what I had been thinking about for a while. He was bright and talented, but poor. If he stayed in the town, that girlfriend might wear him down and get a ring on her finger. I had a cousin who worked at a small college in southern California only surviving by accepting lots of foreign students who could afford the tuition. I had already talked to him about the possibility of getting Miguel a student visa. He could study architecture like he wanted, and I had the power to make it happen.

Six months later the work was winding down. I would have to let some workers go. Miguel had been accepted at the college. I drove him to Mexico City to catch his flight to Los Angeles. We spent the night together in a hotel near the airport, both full of doubt. He clung to me through the darkness, the sounds of jets roaring overhead and the traffic rolling by on the *Periférico*. I didn't sleep as I contemplated giving him up to the great unknown, realizing anything could happen. Yet the closeness we felt that night convinced me nothing could tear us apart, nothing I believed. That was the naiveté of love.

# Cruising

The motorcycle cruised through bands of color along a perfectly flat gray ribbon of road. On either side, fields of tulips were in full bloom, first swaths of red, then yellow, then white, then pink. I came upon a field of flowers that appeared black at first. *Ah, the elusive black tulip.* I pulled over and stopped the bike. On closer examination, they were a velvety deep maroon, almost the exact color of my bike.

I took out a map from the side pocket of my pack. I was near the Dutch town of Lisse, halfway between The Hague and Amsterdam. Though the sun was starting to go down, flooding the fields with gilded light, I didn't think I would have any problem making Amsterdam by dark.

I started my bike and roared onto the road with "Born to be Wild" playing in my head. I had ceased being May Burd, recent graduate Magna Cum Laude from U.C. Berkeley, headed to Stanford Medical School in the fall. I was a bad boy on a hog blazing through the back roads of Europe with no particular goal except to lose track of who I was.

Always an overachiever, I'd graduated early January. I had six months before I would dive into med school and spend the next seven years swimming upstream against a tide of information I would have to absorb. Hard work and physical exertion had never frightened me, but I also relished the chance to take up a challenge of a different sort—being a man on the road, free and independent.

I cut my dark hair short, but still long enough to slick it back behind my ears. I told my hairdresser I didn't care if I looked like a man because I was going to be traveling by myself through Europe and it would be safer. I hadn't told anyone my plan of doing it by motorcycle, though I had a strong desire to tell the person I was closest to, my brother. We had tried to get together several times before I left, but something always got in the way. He was going to school at the University of San Francisco on the other side of the Bay and living in the Haight where he was discovering gay sex—safely I prayed.

Through a catalogue, I ordered a binding garment, which in the description claimed it would flatten my breasts. The morning of the day the package arrived, I woke up and immediately cupped my hands over my breasts, and with a sinking feeling, confirmed they had not diminished as so often happened in a recurring dream. What an encumbrance! They interfered with my golf stroke, my tennis game. I had developed early, my body betraying me and doing it against my will.

I slipped the spandex tank top over my head and tugged the tail down around my hips. The instructions said to reach inside the garment and push my breasts down and to the side. I stood sideways in front of a mirror and couldn't believe my eyes.

I was a stocky man with a developed chest rather than a "big-boned" woman with large breasts. I pulled a black

T-shirt over the undergarment and slipped into a pair of jeans. I worried about my hips looking too wide, but the long top helped in slimming my thighs. My gym routine had kept my tummy flat and my arms strong.

The day I tried on my new binding top was unseasonably warm, making me glad I had chosen early spring as a time to travel in Northern Europe where it was still cool. I could comfortably wear the black motorcycle jacket I bought at a South of Market leather shop in San Francisco. The final touch was a pair of aviator sunglasses.

I stood in front of the mirror trembling. I inhabited a body, not mine but the one I had always wanted. The effect was far beyond any of the feeble attempts I'd made doing male drag for Halloween. One year, a guy I was dating dressed as Bonnie and I was Clyde. We were the hit of the party. But on my trip through Europe, no one would know me. It would not be a joke. I gazed with excitement at my reflection, knowing I could pass. I had even been practicing speaking in a lower register.

After landing in London, I caught a taxi to a shop on the outskirts of the city where they sold used motorcycles. As soon as I saw the maroon Honda ST1100, I knew it was for me. It was masculine without being macho. The seller talked about reliability, comfort, and performance for the long haul. Not ready to tackle London on a bike I wasn't familiar with, I toured southern England along the coast for a few days until I got to Dover. From there, I took the ferry to France, and later got on the road through Belgium to the Netherlands.

A light rain fell as I rode along a canal on the outskirts of Amsterdam. A group of cyclists had stopped to watch several swans paddling near the water's edge. I pulled over as well, took my helmet off, and slicked back my hair. A few of the cyclists turned to look at me with alarm in their eyes. It confused me at first, and then remembering my new image, it pleased me to think I might look like someone to reckon with.

"Hi," I said in a deep voice. "Do you speak English?" It was the last time I had to ask that question. Everybody I met during my time in Holland spoke nearly perfect English.

"Can we help you?" said a pretty blonde woman in her tight hi-tech fabric jersey unzipped as far as it would go. She appeared more daring than the others.

"What is the best way into the old part of Amsterdam?"

Another girl came over. "What is he looking for?"

My heart leapt. People I had interacted with so far were mildly curious, but gave no indication whether they believed I was a man or a woman. The desk clerk on the first night in England at the inn outside Portsmouth glanced at my name on the passport, May Burd. His eyes flashed briefly as if it solved a mystery.

"I'm staying at a hotel on Kerkstraat," I said to the girls. "It faces a canal." I pulled out my map.

The blonde girl traced the directions on my map and gave me a few pointers about avoiding traffic.

"Thank you so much."

"Pleasure," the girl said, sticking out her hand. "I'm Anna."

"Nice to meet you. I'm M...Marlon."

★

I spent the first day in Amsterdam visiting the Van Gogh Museum and the Rijksmuseum. My Jewish ancestors handed down the tradition of culture before fun as if the blood of my people mandated it. And yet every experience, every room in every museum, was fun in my new persona. I was the star of my own work of theater. At the end of the day, I recorded my impressions in a journal: how I felt in my new body; how people who perceived me as a man reacted differently from those who weren't sure; how having a person of questionable gender in any setting changed the dynamic.

Though my plan for the fall was to specialize in child psychiatry, all human behavior fascinated me. And being in Amsterdam, one of the most progressive cities in the world, meant I could push the limits of gender and sexuality with the added benefit I was a stranger here. Many of the characters I observed found a place in my notebook at the end of the day. I wondered if and how I would be portrayed in the notebooks of others.

On the second and third days, I continued being a tourist, taking a canal cruise, strolling through the Red Light District, and trying not to get knocked down by the thousands of bicycles careening through the streets. On the way out of the charming boutique hotel on the third night, I stopped to talk to the young woman behind the desk. With her spiky hair, nose ring, and stars tattooed up her arm, she looked like a person I could ask where to find the marijuana places without either of us feeling uncomfortable.

"First thing," she explained like a teacher, "you need to find a coffeeshop, written as one word, not a coffee shop or café or coffee house. I can recommend a couple."

"Do they have space cake?" I asked. I had tried smoking marijuana a couple of times but found it problematic. I hated smoke and was not fond of anything that slowed my mind. The times I had tried it, I felt stupid for an hour and promptly fell asleep. But a good friend at school had raved about the space cake he had tried in Amsterdam, so I was willing to give edibles a try.

As I stepped out into the cool, drizzly street, I reaffirmed my plan for the evening, the biggest challenge of my trip. I was going to Argos, a men-only leather bar, a place my friend had also talked about. "Too bad you can't go there," he had said. "It's fucking awesome, and so naughty."

I reached into my jacket pocket and touched the accessory I would add to my outfit of leather jacket, T-shirt, jeans, and boots, but was embarrassed to put on before I left the hotel. At a theatrical makeup shop, I had purchased a glue-on mustache labeled "the crime doctor." I loved the name. It allowed me to do anything.

Two hours after I had eaten the space cake, I proclaimed it a dud. If there was the slightest difference in my head, it was because of the glass of wine I had with dinner. I took a deep breath and walked in the door of Argos. The sensation was more like accidentally walking into a men's room, with a distinct odor of urine, beer, and man sweat, than crossing a forbidden portal. It was nearly empty, and people ignored me. I took a seat at the bar and ordered a beer in a bottle, a dark bottle, so no one would notice I was only taking fake sips and not in fact drinking something I found disgusting. The other patrons were clearly leather aficionados, all of them wearing some combination of leather jackets, leather pants, biker caps, and chaps. One skinny, white-haired man was shirtless and wore a harness. I would have a lot to write about in my journal later.

The music was at first a variety of popular songs of the day. I recognized Madonna's "Justify My Love," followed by George Michael's "Freedom." I had never paid much attention to the lyrics of "Freedom," but, at that moment, the words spoke to me. The message of freedom pulled my emotions into a dance, telling me there was something I should know, something deep inside me, something I forgot to be. I shuddered and surveyed the room, wondering if other people were impacted by the words.

The "Freedom" chorus sounded as if a choir of celestial voices had joined Michael, surrounding me with voices from on high, causing a tingling on my skin. My binding made me sweat, and I wanted to take off my jacket. But I didn't, still afraid that somehow my breasts would show. I almost felt something at dinner had disagreed with me, causing this odd sensation. I had completely forgotten about the space cake.

The bar gradually filled up, and the music changed to a more synthesized reverberation with heavy bass and driving percussion. The pounding went directly to my chest. Men were all around me now, some of them staring at me. I was afraid the mustache I applied in the restaurant bathroom was coming loose. They had detected I was not a man. I had no beard, no Adam's apple. I was sweating a lot, and it didn't smell like a man. I was a moment from being discovered and thrown out.

The white-haired man in the harness stood behind

me and whispered in my ear. "Do you want to go downstairs?" My friend had told me about the playroom on the lower level and given graphic details of what went on there.

"Got to finish my beer," I growled. "Maybe later." I was relieved he didn't see me as a woman. Or did he? He turned to his companion and said something in German. They laughed.

Voices swirled around me, lights and shadows constantly changing, the music distorted. My brain kept losing track of where I was, a different country, continent, dimension maybe? I suffered from space cake paranoia. The effects had crept up on me as it was now hours since I'd eaten it. It was powerful, and I didn't like it. I needed fresh air and to get back to the hotel. I stood up and made my way through the crowd.

Outside the door of the bar, I was disoriented and couldn't remember if I was supposed to go left or right, confirming what I disliked about being high, the loss of control. I could have asked plenty of people on the street, but I didn't, afraid if I opened my mouth my words would ring stupid or wouldn't come out. I chose one direction and walked rapidly, regretting I had left my map in the hotel.

I pulled up the collar of my jacket against the cool, damp air. Nothing looked familiar. The streets were soon dark and empty. I heard loud singing in the direction I was walking. As I got closer, I recognized it was English, some kind of rowdy sport song sung by five men in buzz cuts with scarves in team colors and aggressive manners. I crossed the street, hoping they wouldn't see me.

They stopped singing and gawked at me. "Hey,

macho man!" one of them yelled. They were drunk British soccer fans, a bad combination. In this case, I wondered if it was more dangerous to be a woman or perceived as a gay man. I picked up my pace, but they headed in my direction. "Hey, we're talking to you."

"Where you going, faggot?" another said.

"Want to suck my willy, you fucking poofter?" said the one who acted like the ringleader.

Ignore them, I kept telling myself. I heard voices down one street and turned at the corner. They followed.

"Come on, I need a blowie." They were right behind me now.

Though it would behoove me to keep quiet, my anger was about to explode. I turned around. "I probably wouldn't be able to find it." Immediately, I started running toward the other voices I had heard.

I was a good runner, but no match for them. I no longer heard other people, only the senseless shouting of the gang, their words no longer simple profanity but the garbled grunts and growls of animals. They grabbed me and threw me up against the wall.

The leader snarled in my face while the others held me. "We're going to mess you up, fag."

"I'm not a fag," I said in my normal voice.

"Bloody hell," said one of them. "She's a girl."

The leader focused on my mustache. "She's a fucking bull dyke." He tugged at the mustache, and when it gave, he ripped it off my face.

They pushed me into a narrow alleyway. I struggled, managed to elbow one of them. I yelled as loud as I could. They put a hand over my mouth. Their fists pummelled my face. I tasted blood. They pulled my jeans down. I kicked. And then a blow knocked me out.

I woke up in the hospital. One eye was swollen shut. My head throbbed. A woman in white stood over me. "You're safe now. How do you feel?"

"Like shit." They had removed my clothes and put me in a hospital gown. "Did they...did they...?"

The doctor nodded with pursed lips. "I'm sorry. I've ordered a rape kit. Your clothes have been bagged for possible evidence. We believe it was only one of them. Luckily, some guys from a bar nearby arrived before it got any worse and the hoodlums scattered. I guess it was the place where you had been because they said they recognized you."

"Oh," I said and began to sob uncontrollably. I had lost my virginity to a hoodlum who raped me.

"There is a policewoman outside the door who would like to talk to you."

The bruises and cuts were bad enough to need stitches and would take time to heal. The rape would stay with me forever. The policewoman came in and talked to me. I described the young men, but I told her I couldn't stay in town for identification and possible trial. More than anything, I needed to go home. I would not press charges. Though she was sorry about my decision, she said she understood. The young men had most likely already returned to England.

I left the hospital that afternoon. The woman at the hotel helped me sell the bike, though at a significant loss. Two days later, I was on a flight back to San Francisco. I went to the Berkeley apartment where I lived alone and told no one I was home. I stayed there until my wounds healed, only venturing out for food. And I never told anyone what had happened to me in Amsterdam.

I threw myself into med school in the fall. I got rid of the binding garment and with it any thoughts about trying to change or hide the body I was born with. But the feeling that my body wasn't right never left me.

# Venceremos Brigade

Cancun was abuzz with jackhammers, pounding steel, and swinging cranes. From his taxi window Byron saw the skeletons of new hotels emerging from the white sand next to calm azure waters, wide boulevards of bleached concrete ending at the edge of the jungle, and young Mayans in drab, ill-fitting uniforms walking to work along the road. It was "the Mexican miracle of 1980," someone had told him on the plane.

At the Hotel Playa Blanca, he went straight to the pool bar where he drank margaritas, occasionally sticking his finger in the drink to feel the pleasure of cold. The air around him was like hot paste on his skin, and the inside of his brain was on low boil with images of Thomas's face in pain repeatedly rising to the surface. Not the distance nor drugs nor alcohol had managed to quell the guilt he had been responsible for Thomas's death. No amount of self-medicating diminished the rippling sense of loss, the expanding emptiness inside him.

Byron leaned his head down and hovered over the drink, letting the coolness rise to his face. Nearby, a parrot in a cage squawked, as if it, too, was irritated and forlorn.

He felt so very far from home—aimless, drifting. And yet, something in the back of his mind was beginning to take shape. A plan?

A loud voice, sounding as if it had descended from the heavens said, "You part of the boom?"

The only other patron was a man with longish hair and a beard, sitting a few stools down, drinking a Tecate. Byron's thought it an odd way to begin a conversation, and whatever did he mean? It must have been Byron's khaki chinos and blue Oxford cloth long-sleeved shirt that made the man take him for a businessman. His mother was a firm believer in looking one's best for travel. Some things stuck.

Byron turned his heavy eyelids toward the man. "No, sir."

The man chuckled. "So what are you here for?"

Byron was struck by the intrusiveness of the man's question. Had to be a Yankee, probably big city, but Byron's Southern upbringing made it impossible to be rude and not respond. "To escape, I guess."

The man looked Byron up and down. "Can't imagine what you would have to escape from. You get in some trouble at school?"

Byron hesitated a moment, and then answered with a snort. "Oh, yeah, failing grades at college. Not to mention I was witness to my Black friend being shot down in front of me. A bunch of rednecks with rifles threatening to kill me if I came back to town, including one who was a childhood friend. And my daddy telling me to stay away to avoid a scandal."

The man's brow wrinkled, his eyes narrowed, and finally a smiling guess Byron was pulling his leg spread across his face. "Good one," the man said with a laugh. "You must be a Southern writer." He moved closer and extended his hand. "My name's Terry. Hope I'm not intruding. Been in town a couple days and all anybody talks about is the miracle of Cancun."

"Got the same from a guy on the plane."

"Hotels and fast food joints as far as the eye can see," said Terry. "Gonna be worse than Miami Beach."

Byron took the man's hand. "I'm Byron Boudreaux." A chill ran up his spine. It was the first time he had used his mother's maiden name. If he was going to disappear, a name change would be necessary. "Wouldn't Byron Boudreaux be a wonderful name for a writer or an artist?" his aunt had said a few years back. "So much better than your father's name, Purvis. She had always tried to encourage Byron along artistic lines, taking him to cultural events whenever he came to visit, introducing him to a colorful array of New Orleans characters his father would not have approved of.

"I once met a Boudreaux from Louisiana," said Terry. "That where you're from?"

"Mississippi, actually. My mother's from New Orleans though."

"Now that's a great town. Corrupt to its very soul, but at least it's got a soul. This place is a Disneyland."

"If you dislike it so much..." His voice trailed off, not wanting to be further dragged into a personal conversation.

Terry narrowed his pale blues. "You're not CIA, are ya?" He laughed again, a guffaw that set Byron's nerves on edge. "You ever hear of the Venceremos Brigade?"

"Spanish, right? The *venceremos* part."

"It means 'we will win' or 'we shall overcome,' like in the Civil Rights song. In a couple days I'm meeting a group of *brigadistas* from the West coast and we'll sail over to Cuba to do a little work in support of the revolution. I brought my boat down here from Tampa."

Terry continued to stare at him, his face not two feet away. Byron concluded the man was a bore. Why wouldn't he let him get drunk in peace? He wanted nothing more than to get up and walk away, but his upbringing again demanded decorum. Byron sighed. "I thought Cuba was off limits. It's communist, right?"

"Don't make communism sound so much like a disease." Terry reached for his bag and took out a book. It read *Venceremos Brigade: Young Americans Sharing the Life and Work of Revolutionary Cuba*.

"When people ask me that question," Terry continued, "I love to quote this little poem." He opened the book and read. "'Communism is not a religion. I neither believe or disbelieve, nor have I tasted pure water, but I am often thirsty and drink, fight for the springs of the earth'."

The words meant nothing to Byron. "I'm not political myself. One politician in the family is enough. My daddy's running for office in Mississippi."

"Oh, hell, man. Everything is political. Every minute decision we make every day is political. Politics is about power, who's got it and who doesn't.

"But you could go crazy worrying if everything you say or do is politically correct, down to the last detail."

"It's a goal, of course. We're only human. But we've

gotta try. And that's what they're doing in Cuba. Don't take my word for it. Take this book back to your room and read what these people have to say. They were on the first brigades ten years ago. It's not all rosy, but it's honest. Come back and tell me what you think. Maybe you'll want to join us. If you want to escape, escape into something meaningful." Terry stood up, downed the last of his beer, and squeezed Byron's shoulder on the way out of the bar. This was absurd. He would never read it. It was only his inertia that kept him from running after the man and returning the book.

Byron took a sip of his drink and examined the photo on the cover showing a group of men and women of mixed races in a cane field. Byron's eyes fell on the Black men in the picture with their shirts off, and his stomach took a turn. He opened the book and searched for more pictures.

Later at the beach, Byron opened the book to the pages about the work in the fields. The writers described it as grueling, but most of them expressed joy at pushing through to the other side of their pain. Still, Byron found it absurd that Terry had suggested he try this kind of manual labor. The Cuban revolution had nothing to do with him. What could he solve by doing volunteer work on a backwater island whose leader shouted epithets at his native land?

Nevertheless, there were, in addition to the photos, parts of the book that interested him—discussions of Cuba's attempt to build a non-racial society. Though a good part of the population was of mixed race, prejudice had been widespread before the Revolution. It was an issue the revolutionaries addressed, and laws had been passed to create a more equal society. It made him think about the mistrust between Blacks and whites back in

Mississippi. Could Thomas's murder have happened in Cuba? Everything he read, every picture he saw related in some way to Thomas, and each time his heart was stabbed again, the pain bringing tears to his eyes. Was it truly racism that had killed Thomas? Were things better in Cuba? He wavered between thinking the idea of going to Cuba was absurd, and curiosity about a place so unlike home. Could the venture Terry suggested fit somehow into his plan to escape?

When he tired of reading, he again focused on the pictures: a group of exhausted workers in a cane field with machetes dangling at their sides, high-spirited faces on a crowded bus, a meeting around crude tables in a thatch-roofed pavilion. In one photo, two men, one brown and one Black, stared at the camera in defiance, cigarettes hanging from their lips. But their arms were draped over each other's shoulders, and bare torsos leaned together in the kind of intimacy men allow themselves in hard work, sports, and war. Byron was plucked from his suffering, and allowed to float for a mere second on the edge of excitement. In the next moment, the feeling had traveled down to his lower belly and emerged as a twitch of desire. He hastily turned the page.

★

In the hotel lobby Byron ran into Terry. "Byron, my man. Did you get a chance to look at the book?"

"I did. A bit."

"Are you ready to join us?"

"I haven't done much in the way of manual labor. I might have a hard time holding up."

"Don't let the book scare you. They worked the first

*brigadistas* pretty hard. These days it's more about solidarity. We do a couple weeks of cane cutting, and later break up into various groups to do everything from picking fruit to construction. Of course it isn't going to right what's going wrong with you. But there's nothing like hard work to take your mind off problems."

Byron hesitated a moment, distracted by a curly strand of gray that had escaped from Terry's pulled back hair. "You're sailing your boat over? You can do that?"

"Yep." He glided his calloused hand over the air as if it were a boat crossing the sea.

"Do the Cubans share information about comings and goings with U.S. officials?"

"There are no formal relations and the Cubans don't even stamp your passport, just give you a tourist card. Come on. I want you to meet someone. He's Cuban-American, but he doesn't buy into the whole anti-Castro crap."

He led Byron over to an armchair where a handsome, dark-skinned man sat reading, one long, hairy leg draped over the armrest.

"Rafael," said Terry. "This is Byron. He might be joining us."

Rafael's eyes peered over the top of the book as if he were annoyed at being interrupted, but his full lips instantly rose up into a smile. "Oh, we are including movie stars in our groups now?"

Terry laughed, but Byron turned red and felt the urge to slip away. He wasn't accustomed to compliments from men, especially from a man who at first sight confused him. Rafael was a Black man with a foreign accent and an easy style of interaction. He continued to stare unabashedly at Byron, acting as if neither his skin color nor anything about Byron would inhibit him from doing what he wanted.

Terry cleared his throat. "Rafael, give the kid a break."

"Where you from?" asked Rafael.

"Mississippi."

"Por dios, a real live, how you say, cracker man?"

Terry gave Rafael a warning look. "Don't mind him. He had some rather unpleasant experiences traveling through the South."

"Sorry," said Rafael. "I have problem to say everything what come to my head. When we come over in the seventies, my parents they take me to live with an uncle in Miami. Those Miami Cubans are crazy. I had to get out of there. I hitchhiked to San Francisco. Thank God, I find San Francisco. Took me two weeks cause nobody want to pick me up. Can you imagine the people not wanting to give a lift to a handsome devil like me?" His eyes bore into Byron again, making Byron feel like tiny creatures were crawling on his skin.

"You know we're not all racists," Byron said. He wanted to announce to the whole lobby where his hands and lips had been, that he relished Black skin, the feel and taste of it. That proved he wasn't racist, didn't it? Instead he lowered his eyes. "But I know what you mean." In thinking about Thomas, his blue eyes glistened and his jaw quivered slightly.

"Seems like I make you sad," said Rafael. "Sorry."

"I guess nobody likes to be stereotyped."

"You're absolutely right. Anyway, sit down. Talk with me."

"I'll leave you in Rafael's care," Terry said to Byron. "I've got stuff to do." And to Rafael, "Be nice."

Rafael explained why he had joined the brigade and what it meant to do something for his homeland rather than scream and moan like many of his fellow Cuban-Americans did.

"I love my country. I only come to States because my parents bring me. I think there is much good with Revolution."

Byron was mesmerized by Rafael's voice, the extraordinary accent, his penetrating eyes that shined when he told Byron how the brigade worked hard, but played hard, too. And Rafael claimed to know all the places where they could have fun. Several times he touched Byron's arm while he was talking, and a couple of times broke into a laughter, making heads turn in the lobby. Rafael wasn't like anyone he knew back in Mississippi.

★

In the dark, Byron and Rafael clambered onto Terry's thirty-five-foot Pearson yawl. By the time they were out of the bay, calm waters reflected a rosy dawn. Terry was at the wheel, and his crew, Maggie and Jason, were perched on either side of the cabin. Byron leaned over the stern railing and lost himself in the gentle wake, thin white trails gradually dissipating. A sense of peace, almost allowed him to let go of the events that had battered him in the past week. With the crest of each wave he got farther and farther away from the horrible events back home.

Byron declined the Dramamine. He had never had a hint of seasickness, though he forgot to take into account that his experience on boats had been limited to calm waters—his father's fishing boat and canoes on the river. Two hours after leaving shore, he was stretched out on the deck bench, his pounding head resting on Rafael's thigh while saltwater sprayed over the side and the mainsail popped and fluttered. He had spent the second hour vomiting until there was nothing left. Rafael mopped the sweat from his brow with a damp washcloth; the intimacy felt awkward, soothing, and exciting all at once. Already, he enjoyed a peculiar ease with Rafael he had never had with Thomas.

Until Rafael had come along, no one had comforted him. He hadn't been able to talk to anybody about his agony—neither his Aunt Lidia nor his mother nor friends at school. Rafael's kindness and simple flirtations didn't lead him out of his hell, but made it slightly more tolerable.

In the afternoon, Byron's stomach had settled enough he was able to keep a Dramamine down, and he crawled into a berth to sleep. Sometime in the night Rafael slipped into the bed they had to share. He gave Byron a brotherly kiss on the back of his head and threw a protective arm over his back. In the morning he felt better until they told him it would be at least another twenty-four hours before they arrived in Havana.

The following day around noon they docked in Marina Hemingway near Havana. Byron tested his wobbly legs on the dock, looking around at the marina full of boats sporting an assortment of flags, including American, Canadian, Mexican, Spanish, and Venezuelan.

The five of them hired a taxi, a 1952 Chevy, to take them into the center of Havana where they would spend one night before the bus took them to their work camp early the next morning.

The car bumped and rattled along Avenida Quinta toward Havana, and the poor suspension along with the tired seat springs caused them to bounce up and down as they gazed out the windows. Byron and Rafael were pressed together in the back seat—they had taken on a sixth passenger soon after getting on the highway—and their legs rubbed together, causing sweat to run from their knees down to their ankles.

They saw many other American cars from the fifties—nothing after 1959, the year the revolutionaries took control of the government—alongside later model cars manufactured in the Soviet Union and Eastern Europe. While Terry and the others marveled at the cars, Byron focused on the people. Cubans of every skin color, from Black African to pale European and everything in between, walked along the road and sometimes stuck out their hands, wiggling them to solicit rides. Others rode bicycles, often with two or three people on a single bike. At bus stops, men, women, and children waited with expressions and postures of resignation as if it could be a long time before the bus showed up. Poverty was evident in their clothes, the number of simple structures needing repairs or a coat of paint, and the poor infrastructure. And yet, the people didn't look unhappy. Women swayed their hips, men strutted, and children laughed.

Terry had a reservation at the Habana Libre, the pre-revolution Havana Hilton, located off La Rampa in Vedado. Byron offered to pay for a room in the same hotel if Rafael wanted to join him. "A room with two beds," Byron added with a tight jaw.

Rafael grinned. "As you like, *señor*. I only agree because I know you need help in this new city—the new places, the new food, everything. Don't worry. You can count on me."

"Soak up the luxury, boys, before we descend into Hades." Terry laughed with his belly and slapped Byron on the back. Byron wrinkled his forehead and squinted in a stunned look of an old man. People closest to him frequently teased him about it.

The following morning a group of about a hundred *brigadistas*, plus a large number of Cubans who would be joining them at the work camps, assembled at the Plaza de la Revolution alongside a string of old buses, many of them donated by Canada, Venezuela, and Mexico. They were flanked by the giant statue of Martí on one side of the Plaza, and the steel silhouette of the iconic Che portrait attached high up on the Ministry of the Interior.

"Do you not feel the eyes of these two great revolutionary figures smiling down on us?" said Rafael.

Byron nodded, the stunned look still on his face. What the hell was he doing? It was bad enough he was breaking U.S. laws by being in Cuba, but associating with revolutionaries? His original idea of disappearing had morphed into something bigger, more otherworldly, and questionably the decision of a sane mind. But he had to admit no one would search for him here.

Rafael leaned close to Byron and whispered the two men in berets standing next to him were Black Panthers. On seeing Byron's expression, he squeezed his shoulder and laughingly said, "Don't worry. I protect you."

Of the hundreds of people milling about the plaza, there were men already in work clothes and others looking like they were about to spend a day at the beach: white girls wearing straw hats and overalls, Black girls wearing bandanas and tight shorts, men and women of every skin color, most of them smiling in awe. A rumor weaved through the crowd Fidel might stop by to see them off. Though Byron pretended none of it mattered to him, he was genuinely disappointed the Man didn't make an appearance.

When Byron had gazed out the scratched windows of the bus the previous afternoon, he found the cane fields of Matanzas Province beautiful, a sea of brilliant green, the stalks upright with lazy tops swaying in the wind. Now he stood in the middle of those fields between the thick, tight clumps, each one growing from a mound of soil. Up close its jointed stalks reminded him of bamboo; in addition to the green, parts of the plant were yellow and red, revealing nature's bounty.

Rafael stood over Byron and instructed him how to cut the cane. "Take machete firmly in hand, better not to use gloves. Well, okay, maybe use gloves. Put the leg opposite the machete, hand well forward. Step up and whack the stalk like you mean it. Maybe you want to imagine it is the devil of your dreams."

"What do you know about my dreams?"

"I heard you last night in the hotel. Was tempted to go comfort you, but you were so sure about the two bed thing."

Byron looked around to see if anybody was listening.

"You can talk to me, you know," Rafael continued. "You don't have to keep it inside." He leaned over Byron, slid his arm along Byron's, and grabbed his wrist. "Now with a quick, down motion, strike the stalk at ground level, cutting it from its Mama Earth. If you leave stumps, it maybe makes the rot and grow back wrong. Yank the stalk up, cut it into lengths of about four or five feet, and cut off the leafy top. Throw the stalks behind you and someone will pile them. Keep moving. Try to keep even with your partners in the next row. That's all there is to it. Now you try it."

Byron aimed the blade and slammed it into a thick clump of stalks. The machete stuck in a stalk and his hand came away empty. Rafael chuckled and shook his head.

"Shut up," said Byron. He grabbed the machete, pulled it out, and swung heavily into the clump.

"Watch your leg!" screamed Rafael.

The cane toppled over, but Byron came within an inch of lopping off his left kneecap in the follow-through.

"*Por Diós*, By! Be careful!" Byron shook at being called By. The only other person who had done it was Thomas.

It took Byron most of the morning to be able to make a clean cut. Sweat dripped down in his eyes and his hands were numb. The muscles of his back burned like ropes on fire. The physical exertion was beyond anything he had ever experienced, and he also had to deal with the added pressure that Malik, one of the Black Panthers they had seen earlier, was his crew boss. As Byron fell behind in his row, Malik sauntered over and gave him an intimidating stare. At first Byron cringed and forced himself to work harder. But then he stopped and let out a snigger. The irony of the scene hit hard: He was the blond Southern aristocrat doing the backbreaking work of the enslaved while a Black man watched over him.

"What's so funny, Boudreaux?"

Byron was shocked Malik knew his name. "Nothing," said Byron, and he slammed the machete as hard as he could into a thick stalk. It toppled over.

By the time they broke for the long lunch and siesta to avoid the hottest part of the day, Byron was so drained he skipped the dining hall, went to the barracks, and flopped on his lower bunk. Rafael came in with a plate of food. "You gotta eat. You need strength for the afternoon."

"What afternoon? I'm done." He rolled over and faced the wall.

Rafael took him by the shoulder and gently shook him. "Come on. You'll get it. Each day gets better, and soon we are finish before you know it."

Byron shook off his hand. "I don't need you to take care of me. This was a mistake. I don't know what I'm doing here." His voice cracked from exhaustion and pent-up emotion. He bit his lip to stop the flow of tears.

"Is okay, *amigo*. But you need to eat something."

"What I need is for you to leave me alone."

Rafael returned his hand to Byron's back and rubbed it. "I'm only trying to help. Talk to me."

"Stop it! Shit! What if somebody comes in?" His sharp words belied the comfort Rafael's compassion brought him. Someone cared about him. His body began to shake.

"Hey, come on. Don't do that." Rafael now had his

hand on Byron head, smoothing his hair.

The screen door slammed shut and Malik came in, trudged past them, staring hard at Rafael.

"What are you looking at?" said Rafael.

"That shit got no place here."

"And what shit you talking about? Comforting a *compañero* who's down? No human kindness in your kinda revolution?"

"You know what I'm talking about. The Cuban Revolution put people like you in camps for a little re-education."

"You don't know the history. The Cuban government, including Fidel, recognized the UMAP camps were wrong and they are closed a long time ago."

"If you ask me, they oughta bring 'em back, them camps, teach people how to act proper."

"Well, nobody ask you." Rafael wasn't a big man, about five-nine, a hundred and sixty pounds. But he didn't back down. The Panther, who had several inches and about forty pounds on Rafael, walked toward his bunk, looking over his shoulder a couple of times with a sneer. Malik got his clipboard and walked out.

Rafael hanging tough with a Panther impressed Byron, made him sit up and wipe his eyes. "You don't care what people think, do you?" said Byron.

"I care about what people I care about think."

Byron produced a half-smile. "Not sure you'd care about me if you knew what I'm thinking about."

"Try me."

"Revenge." The word, elongated and frightening, rose up from deep in his gut. It was the first time he had uttered the word out loud.

"Don't worry about that guy. He have to maintain an image."

"Not him. Something much bigger."

Since that day in the woods, vengeance had consumed Byron, a slow burn like pages of a book going from yellow to red, curling up into a delicate black ash. But the pages kept rising. For each level of hurt that drifted upward there was one beneath to replace it. He had the guilt of a survivor and the righteous anger of the wronged. But he was weak, had never even been in a fight, at least nothing more than a childish shoving match. Why couldn't he learn to be a warrior like Rafael? It wasn't impossible. His training could start with the challenge of cane cutting. Two weeks of it wouldn't make him a warrior, but it could be a start. He saw it now. He would get stronger day by day. He would not cry again. Nothing in his short indulgent life had prepared him for this, but people could change, couldn't they?

With this realization he went back out in the fields in the afternoon and every day after, even when he was filthy, sweaty, sick, exhausted, lower back screaming, and whole parts of his body numb. He learned to work through the pain because now he had a goal: to lose the genteel person he was raised to be, and become a person who fought for what he wanted. At times his eyes rose to see Rafael in the next row, staring at him with a look of consternation on his face, witness to a metamorphosis.

★

In the evenings, the workers had meetings where they talked about the day's problems, listened to a report on the yield, and discussed politics. In the years since the first brigade made a significant contribution to the 1970 *zafra,* or harvest, in its goal to reach ten million tons, the focus of cutting cane had shifted to a more psychological and social contribution than an economic one. The meetings were part of educating the workers so they would go back to their respective countries and inform people about what was happening in Cuba.

Near the end of the first week, after an exhausting day of cutting, the best in terms of yield, the sunburned workers trudged into the meeting room. Some of them had bandaged hands and others limped, but on many faces was the satisfaction of making a contribution to something they believed in. The meeting moved to the open discussion portion. Rafael indicated he had something to say and stood up. Byron, sitting next to him, cringed; he had a premonition of the topic Rafael was going to bring up. Since the day Malik had implied they belonged in a reeducation camp, Rafael had broached the topic many times. "Who does he think he is?" Rafael would say to Byron. "They want revolution, but they want it their way, their terms."

"*Compañeros,*" Rafael began, "I would like to know why some people believe the gay people cannot be revolutionaries. Is not a revolution about changing the old order and eliminating discrimination in all forms? This new socialist man that everybody talks about seems to have new ideas about everything except gay people."

Silence fell on the room like a dark cloud with a storm tucked inside it. Malik swung around in an exaggerated motion and glared at Rafael. "What? You really want to talk about this shit?"

"Language, Malik," said the moderator, a tall sandy-haired woman who was the camp doctor.

"Yeah, all right," said Malik. "But come on. Comparing what the Black man has had to endure to the plight of the homosexual? Man, it's not even in the same ballpark."

The air in the room crackled with murmurs. Byron's face went hot, and now Malik's tough stare fell on him rather than Rafael. Byron gripped his seat and his anxious heart thumped. He had never heard the word "homosexual" uttered in a public forum. Even the private talks he had had with Rafael left him distraught. Rafael kept telling Byron he shouldn't let his emotions stew in his gut or they would boil over. With Thomas they had never talked about their feelings, and being with him had been a ride down a river of white rapids, an emotional run that swiftly reached beyond what his brain could put into words. Rafael's openness posed new complexities: the anxiety of facing who he was mixed with the guilt he was on the edge of being untrue to Thomas. Any attempt Byron made to understand his feelings always arrived at the simple equation: Following your heart equaled death.

And yet he admired Rafael's courage, asserting his right to be who he was in the face of people like Malik. Rafael stood strong, and the moderator asked for silence. Rafael continued, looking straight at Malik. "You know the Nazis kill not only millions of Jews, but also hundreds of thousands of homosexuals."

A young Cuban man, a representative of Juventud Rebelde, rose to speak. "Of course is wrong the killing of homosexuals, but we in Cuba see the homosexual is concerned only with himself and his desires. This way he can't be a revolutionary. We do not hate him and we invite him to be with us in the Revolution, but he wants only his own world and not be part of good for everybody." Several people nodded and mouthed their approval.

The next to speak was a woman whose nasal vowels pegged her as a New Yorker. "I would like to make two points, if I might. First, why is the topic of homosexuality always dominated by the discussion of gay men, always using the pronouns 'he' and 'him'? And while we're at it, isn't it time we start talking about the 'new person' rather than the 'new man'? I have been in the revolution movement since the late sixties and have been involved in every group you can name. Believe me, lesbians have played a huge role in every organization I know." She turned to look directly at Malik. "And I have known more than a few gay sisters in the Panthers, including a prominent figure whose name I won't mention. But again, nobody wants to talk about lesbians or even the closeted gay men who pass for straight. Men are obsessed with the out and sometimes effeminate man."

"Right on, *compañera!*" said a petite Black woman who Byron had observed whacking cane stalks with the force of someone twice her size. "Once I heard brother Huey Newton talk about the urge of a man to hit the homosexual in the mouth and the tendency to make women shut up in the same breath. He said it stemmed from a man's insecurities, fear he might be a homosexual himself, and in the case of women, that he felt castrated. Newton advocated for both women and homosexuals being considered oppressed groups, and that the women's rights and gay rights movements must be part of the Black man's fight for freedom from oppression. I remember him distinctly saying not only could a homosexual be a revolutionary, but the most revolutionary."

A wave of surprise serpentined through the room and arguments rose among the various groups. Some of them had probably known Huey from his years in Cuba, where he had fled prosecution for a murder.

All eyes turned to the front of the room when the camp doctor rose to speak. "This does not surprise me at all, the words of *compañero* Huey. When I am not a camp doctor, I teach at the University of Havana Medical School. These negative attitudes toward homosexuals I see all the time among my students. I remind them they will be doctors and are sworn to help people. Prejudice against homosexuals, like treating women as inferiors, is machismo, pure and simple, and it has no place in a socialist society. I do feel we are on the verge of changing our outdated opinions in this country, but machismo dies hard."

Malik had turned back toward the front, his arms crossed over his chest, head down. He appeared to listen intently, but with his shoulders slightly arched. Rafael had told Byron Malik was one of the Panthers who got into trouble with the police back home and fled to Cuba like Huey Newton. Now he worked as an organizer of foreign groups. Malik swore he would never go home and stand trial the way Huey had. Seeing him now, defeated, in a place he maybe didn't want to be, made Byron feel a surprising pang of sympathy.

The following Saturday was only a half day of work and they had Sunday off. By one o'clock Byron and Rafael were on a local bus that took them into Cárdenas, a town of low buildings, bicycles, and horse-drawn carriages nestled on the Cárdenas Bay, which in turn was protected by a finger of land jutting out into the Caribbean. That lean peninsula, Varadero, was their destination. They changed buses at the terminal and headed out the Via Blanca highway, arriving at the white sand beaches and aquamarine sea of what had been a playground for the rich in the fifties.

A taxi took them to the Kawana hotel—not the finest in the area, but a decadent luxury after the conditions at the camp. At the front desk, two women sat behind the counter. They glanced up at the boys, and promptly went back to their conversation, which had the ease of gossip rather than work.

Rafael drummed his fingers on the counter and said, "*Hola?*"

"*Un momento, por favor, señores.*"

The women continued to ignore them, speaking in low voices, peppering their conversation with expressions of surprise: *No me digas!* and *No puede ser!* Rafael and Byron turned their attention to a blond, shirtless young man, burnt to an inch of his life, flip-flopping through the lobby. Rafael arched his eyebrows at Byron, who immediately turned to look back at the women behind the counter. The women still conversed in a languorous world where even the ceiling fans rotated at the speed of a merry-go-round a parent had tired of pushing.

A few more moments passed before one of the women rose to her feet with some effort and sauntered over to them, looking first at Rafael, then Byron. Her face transitioned from carefree to the steely gaze of a party member. At home she was probably in the local

Committee for the Defense of the Revolution, volunteers who made sure all the neighbors were adhering to the principles of the revolution.

"*Sí?*" She drew out the word as if it were several syllables instead of one.

"We'd like a room," Rafael said in forceful Spanish.

The woman glanced at her co-worker, and then back at them. "Together?"

"Of course," said Rafael.

"You're Cuban, right?" Cubans always recognized other Cubans. The accent was a giveaway.

"Yes."

"Well, then you should know it's not possible."

Rafael stared her down, not in a nasty way, but rather in amusement. In the short time Byron had known him, he recognized when Rafael was having fun with people, keeping them guessing. At times he enthusiastically supported the Revolution, the parts he agreed with, but laughed about the parts that didn't make sense. The co-worker got up and stood next to her friend. Her uniform blouse was a size too small and revealed her bra in the gap between buttons.

"There's a hotel down the road for Cubans. Your friend can stay here," said the other woman.

"What's going on?" Byron's Spanish was still too weak to follow the conversation.

"She wants to separate us in different hotels. What do you think of that?"

"Let's go," said Byron.

To the women Rafael said, "See, you've upset my

friend, a fine tourist from *el yuma*." Cubans often referred to the United States as *el yuma*, though Byron hadn't been able to find someone who could explain why. "But I think we can resolve this." He reached in the pocket of his backpack, pulled out his passport, and slammed it on the counter, making the women start.

"*Soy Cubano con pasaporte Americano!*"

They stared at the passport like he had just produced a letter personally signed by Fidel Castro. Even the staunchest revolutionaries had a touch of envy when they saw a passport that could open thousands of doors for them. But they hastily recovered and forced a smile. "Why didn't you say so?" one of them said in good English.

"With a sea view, please, upper floor," said Rafael.

Rafael jangled the key in his hand and draped his arm over Byron's shoulders as they walked to their room. As soon as they had unlocked the door, Rafael looked at the two beds that had been pushed together and said, "I like it." Byron experienced a dead weight in his stomach and moved hurriedly toward the arched door leading out to the balcony.

"Look at this," he said, throwing the door open and stepping out on the tiled area with a table and two rattan chairs. They had a view of the giant swimming pool and, beyond that, the tranquil deep blue of the sea, edged in a beach so white it looked like snow.

Later at the beach they kicked up sugary sand and dove into warm water that Rafael described as the color of Byron's eyes. They lay side by side, nearly touching, and no one seemed to mind. On the way back to the hotel, they came upon an impromptu street party. It happened anyplace there was a boom box playing salsa, a bottle of rum, and hips that longed to move, which was most everywhere in Cuba.

Byron watched a girl, perhaps five years old, moving her body to the music of Cuba's perennial pop group, Los Van Van. She wore a skimpy halter-top, shiny red nylon shorts, and sandals with big plastic sunflowers on the toes. She danced as if she were born to do it, her body attached by invisible strings to the music. The girl's parents stood by smiling as she swayed and gyrated and spun, out-dancing the teenagers and adults around her. At such a tender age she knew how to move her body in the world without the slightest hesitancy to do so. She was remarkable for her age, but all the Cubans who danced around the crackly speakers cranked up to maximum volume—svelte and squat, old and young, wearing clothes tattered or new from Miami—had the same sensuality, owning his or her little square of broken concrete, saying, "I'm here, look at me."

Rafael brought that same sense of self and lack of shame back to the room as heat lightning streaked the late-afternoon sky. Byron stood at the window, his back to the room and its possibilities, and focused on a place far out at sea. Rafael came up behind Byron, wrapped his arms around him, and wedged his nose behind Byron's ear. He inhaled deeply. "This is the spot. It is beautiful, this sweet smell of Byron."

Byron tensed. "I really don't think..."

"Shhh," Rafael breathed into his ear, sending a cascade of pure oxygen down Byron's spine.

"I can't."

"Yes, you can and you want."

Byron's half-hearted resistance was no match for Rafael's charm, the beers they had been drinking all afternoon, and the sultry air of Cuba infusing everything with sensuality.

Later, when they collapsed in a tangle of sweaty limbs, it was as if Byron had enjoyed sex for the first time, sex in its three stages: teasing foreplay, a desperate animalistic fucking followed by a gentle rocking embrace.

There was something perfect about the way Rafael cradled him while a salty ocean breeze made the sheer curtain dance in the copper light of sunset. Rafael sighed contentedly in his ear, one arm over his chest and a leg on top of Byron's, creating maximum skin-on-skin contact. He played with the few hairs on Byron's chest until he fell into the heavy breathing of sleep. And yet, it was not perfect. Shame latched onto Byron like a leech, sucking out all the joy. That was nothing new. But now it was combined with the notion that pleasure was not due him as long as Thomas's ghost roamed the Earth looking for justice.

★

Instead of going over to where he usually sat with Rafael on afternoon breaks, Byron collapsed on the ground near Malik, rubbing his sore legs. He took off his bandana and wrung it out, forming a puddle in the dirt.

"You were cutting really hard today," said Malik. "You trying to prove something?"

"Nah," said Byron.

"Maybe you're trying to impress your friend who, by the way, keeps looking over at us. I think he's jealous."

Byron laughed, but he was baffled. In a week, Malik had gone from hateful stares to teasing comments. It was partly the camaraderie of the Brigade that demanded it—they were all in the work together. And since that meeting where Rafael had broached the subject of gay revolutionaries, the majority had agreed that they had to respect one another, no matter their differences. At the same time Byron wondered if Malik was as down on homosexuals as he professed. Sometimes out in the fields or across the meeting room, Byron would feel eyes on him and look up to see Malik staring—not hateful staring, but curious. Their eyes would meet for a second, and then Malik would turn his head.

"You ever kill anybody?" Byron asked.

Malik twisted his lips to one side and gazed up at the murky sky. "Don't rightly know. I was in a shootout once. I had a gun in my hand and fired it. There were bullets flying ever which way. We escaped. The next day we read in the newspaper one of the cops took a slug and died at the hospital. That's when it was clear I had to leave. I came here."

"But if you knew you killed him, how would you feel?"

"They were shooting to kill. Plenty brothers have lost their lives at the hands of the pigs. So what? If you worried your revenge is going to run up against your moral fiber, you better forget it right now. We didn't ask for a fight. They brung it to us. And you didn't ask for your fight." Malik paused and used his hand to wipe the sweat from his face. "Ya know, there's something you ain't telling me."

"What do you mean?"

"What were you and that brother doing out there in the woods? I mean, there are plenty of crazy-ass honkies that'll blow a Black man away for no good reason, but you said y'all were just fishing. Really?"

Byron had spared him the sexual details both because he didn't think Malik could handle it, and he didn't want to say it out loud. Now Malik was practically begging for it. His eyes dropped to the ground and he spoke in a quiet voice. "I had let my hair grow long. From a distance, they thought I was a girl."

"What? Shit! There ain't nothing they hate more than a brother messing with their white women. I guess second would probably be queers. In this case they sorta killed two birds with one stone. Of course, you're still alive 'cause you're white."

"There was a moment I wished they'd shot me, too."

Malik twisted his lips. "But they didn't. That's the point. Shit."

★

Descending from the treetops, the call of the cicadas circled him in a tightening grip. And just as the cacophony was about to squeeze the life from him, the tumult elongated, changing from a deafening hum to a chorus of celestial voices, an ethereal repetition of a two-note melody. Pressed to the ground, the bitter green of the grass smarted his eyes, the scent of earth, its decay and rebirth shooting up his nostrils and exploding in his brain. The magnolia tree above him was filled with the winged red-eyed males, shaking their tymbals like there was no tomorrow. With a gust of wind came a sudden crack: a thick branch snapping of its own weight began its descent with great speed toward him. He needed to move, but the incubus pressed down on him, sending him into a panic of labored breathing and voiceless shouts. But instead of crashing down on him, the branch was stopped by something or someone.

His mother's face danced in front of him—the way she looked that day in the Town Car so many years before, her chestnut-colored eyes full of fear and her lips warning of the curse of the cicadas. He sensed the weight still on top of him, felt the hot viscous liquid dripping down his sides. With a trembling gloved hand his mother brushed his side and put her fingers in front of his face. The kidskin gloves were smeared with blood. "See?" she said.

"Help me, Mama," he whimpered.

His eyes opened to the gurgle of his own weeping, and he clambered to consciousness. He touched the stickiness on his chest. It wasn't scarlet like in his dream, but rather sweat pooling in every crevice of his torso.

The terrifying dream had haunted him since the day Thomas was killed. Each time he awoke he remembered what had been taken from him: the days when love was sweet and birds sang and the sun fell through the leaves in dappled patterns on their backs. That memory immediately prompted a question: how could he get justice for Thomas?

Over the last few weeks Byron had awakened from the dream in so many different places that it took time each morning to orient himself. He sat upright and surveyed his surroundings. Ah, a studio apartment in Barcelona. He had gone from New Orleans to Mexico to Cuba, and now Spain. His meandering, at times seemingly without purpose, held a certain logic in each move, if not a carefully designed plan.

When the *brigadistas* had returned to Havana before

their next work assignments, he and Rafael had again shared a hotel room. Byron stole away in the middle of the night and got on a flight to Barcelona, the city he had most enjoyed on his brief senior-year trip through Europe. He took one last look at Rafael's sleeping body, still fresh from their love making, covered by a white sheet. He left no message behind, no parting kiss, no promises to keep in touch. He felt the wretch for abandoning Rafael, who had been so good to him, supportive without question, and loved him without expecting love in return. Rafael's endearing qualities, which at first had bolstered Byron, over time threatened to drown him. Since he fled Havana, he had his moments of loneliness and panic, moments when he regretted his decision, but it couldn't be undone.

# Acknowledgements

"We *Are* the Revolution" was first published in *WITH: New Gay Fiction*. Thanks to editor, Jameson Currier, for including my story in this collection.

"Blade of Grass" was first published in *Best Gay Erotica of the Year, Volume 4*. Thanks to editor, Rob Rosen, for including my story in this collection.

Thanks to the people of Barcelona for giving me a home for five years and a special place in my heart forever. And to all the millions of people who have suffered from Covid-19, I dedicate, "Shelter in Place."

Thanks to my friends in the graduating class of MacArthur High School in Decatur, Illinois who encouraged me to attend the fifty-year reunion and gave me lots of love and support. "Reunion" was inspired by my trip back to the hometown.

"Man in a Shalwar Kameez," "Market Day in Qatif," and "Manama Christmas" were all inspired by my time in Saudi Arabia teaching English. Parts of these stories have been loosely adapted from my first novel, *Eddie's Desert Rose*. "Manama Christmas" is dedicated to all those women who, for better or worse, fall in love with gay men and, in some cases, marry them.

"All in the Cuban Family" received an honorable mention from *Glimmer Train*. It is adapted from my novel *Down in Cuba*.

"Backlit" was inspired by a tragic story I read in the news.

"Miguel Mio" is in part adapted from my novel *Tio Jorge*. My trips to the magical country of Mexico have influenced my writing in many ways.

"Cruising" the only story in the collection not focusing on gay men, is adapted from my novel *Four Calling Burds*. The character will reappear in an upcoming novel.

"Venceremos Brigade" also takes place in Cuba and is adapted from my novel *Deluge*.

I want to thank all the wonderful people I have met in my travels throughout the world. You have filled me with inspiration to write my stories.

Special gratitude to my loving husband, Robert, who gives me strength to do what I do. Though he didn't accompany me on the travels that inspired this collection, he has become in recent years my dedicated companion in exploring the world.

# About Vincent Traughber Meis

Vincent Traughber Meis is a member of the San Francisco Bay Area writing community. He has been a community college teacher, an editor, and a world traveler. His writings include novels, short stories, and travel articles. He was a co-creator of the imprint Fallen Bros Press where he has published his five previous novels. Three of these novels have received Rainbow Awards. His writings have appeared in magazines and short story collections. He lives in San Leandro, California with his husband.

Email
vtmeis@sbcglobal.net

Facebook
www.facebook.com/vincent.meis

Twitter
convince415

Website
www.vincentmeis.com

## Other NineStar books by this author

*The Mayor of Oak Street*

# Also from NineStar Press

## The Mayor of Oak Street by Vincent Traughber Meis

In the 1960s, Midwestern boy and Boy Scout, Nathan delivers newspapers and mows lawns. Nathan uses his cover to move about yards and sneak into the homes of his neighbors, uncovering their secrets.

In high school, one of the local misfits introduces him to diet pills, which help him overcome his shyness. In an amphetamine high, he meets Cindy, who he hopes will steer him along the "morally straight" path of the Boy Scout Oath he swore to.

Nathan is infatuated with a young doctor down the street, Nicholas (Dr. B), who embodies all the things his mother would love him to be. On one of his secret forays in Dr. B's house, he hides in a closet and witnesses his idol having sex with man while the wife is out of town. Dr. B's affair leads to tragedy, forcing the doctor to leave town. At college in New Orleans, Nathan meets a group of rebels and expands his drug use. Marc, a bisexual Cajun charmer becomes Nathan's first male sexual experience, but promptly leaves town.

Nathan has a chance encounter with Dr. B, who has moved to New Orleans. Dr. B is in a relationship, but still closeted. Frustrated by Dr. B's cool reaction, Nathan goes on a six-month binge of amphetamines and anonymous sex. On one night of debauchery, he overdoses and ends up in the emergency ward.

Nathan's near death rallies Dr. B and Nathan's other friends to force him into rehab. On the way home from work, Nathan witnesses the gruesome aftermath of the 1973 Up Stairs Lounge fire that devastated the gay population of New Orleans. As a result of the fire, Dr. B's live-in boyfriend leaves town, freeing Dr. B to explore his feelings for Nathan.

## Connect with NineStar Press

www.ninestarpress.com

www.facebook.com/ninestarpress

www.facebook.com/groups/NineStarNiche

www.twitter.com/ninestarpress

www.instagram.com/ninestarpress